THE BOLD AND THE BANISHED

GOOD TO THE LAST DEMON

BOOK 3

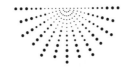

ROBYN PETERMAN

ACKNOWLEDGMENTS

The Bold and the Banished is book 3 in a spinoff of The Good To The Last Death Series. You don't have to have read the other series, but there are fun shout outs for those who have. Candy Vargo makes a big appearance in this one.

I wrote The Facts of Midlife knowing I was going to spin Abaddon off into his own series.
And then I came up with the perfect heroine.

I promised myself a very long time ago that someday I would write a story about an actress and use some of my real life experiences...
That time has come. LOL
The names have been changed to protect the innocent and the guilty.

The situations have been slightly altered.
Clearly, I'm not a Demon—well not on a daily basis.
Cecily, our new and fabulous heroine, is a Demon.

So get ready for a wild, wild ride. I had a blast writing The Bold and the Banished and hope you love reading about Abaddon and Cecily.

As always, writing may be a solitary sport, but it takes a bunch of terrific people to get a book out into the world.

Renee — Thank you for my beautiful cover and for being the best badass critique partner in the world. TMB. LOL

Wanda — You are the freaking bomb. Love you to the moon and back.

Heather, Nancy, Susan, Caroline and Wanda — Thank you for reading early and helping me find the booboos. You all saved my ass. You rock.

My Readers — Thank you for loving the stories that come from my warped mind. It thrills me.

Steve, Henry and Audrey — Your love and support makes all of this so much more fun. I love you people endlessly.

DEDICATION

For my brother Sean. Miss you everyday.

MORE IN THE GOOD TO THE LAST DEMON SERIES

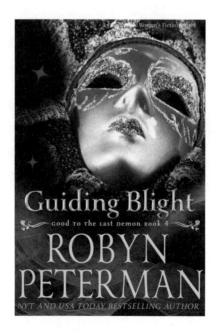

BOOK DESCRIPTION

THE BOLD AND THE BANISHED

My motto—Let's get this party started. My goal—staying alive.

Recently, I was given my own sitcom and my forties were looking fabulous. My dreams were finally coming true —*were* being the operative word.

Of course, just when I think I might have a grip on my newly discovered Demon status, it all goes to Hell. Literally.

I've gone from enemies-to-lovers back to enemies with the hottest Demon alive, who also happens to be the producer on my show. What I'd like to do is never see Abaddon's stupidly handsome face again.

Too bad, so sad. I need his help. The evil whack-job Pandora has kidnapped someone who I love and adore. That's not working for me. At all.

With a grenade carrying Succubus, an Angel with a penchant for blue lipliner, a Demon with bigger boobs than sense, and Abaddon on my team, I'm going into the Darkness to save someone I can't live without.

I have no clue what's coming next, but as an actress I'm not afraid to go method. I've already cried my river of tears and built a bridge to get over it. I'll cross it as a badass as I face my Immortal enemy, because in my line of work, fortune favors the Bold.

***The Good To The Last Demon Series is a spinoff of the Good To The Last Death Series.

CHAPTER ONE

My world was going to Hell in a handbasket in a literal way. I'd effectively blown up my love life with Abaddon since I wanted to be loved for me and not by someone under a compulsion to want me. Demons might look at things differently, but I had forty human years under my belt and only a few weeks of being aware of my Demon heritage.

And what a few weeks it had been.

Trying to avoid being killed and keeping my dad and brother safe had become my full time job. Living a double life as a human actress and a very reluctant Demon Goddess was complicated. Whatever. It was what it was.

And now? Now I was doing something else I didn't want to do.

Outside the restaurant, I gripped my trusty truck, Judy's steering wheel and debated not going through with dinner. There were paparazzi everywhere. It made me itchy. I had no clue who was at the restaurant to cause such a fuss. I was tempted to text Slash and make up a lie to get out of it, but I'd just have to reschedule. Slash might be lacking in the brains department, but my ex-husband was persistent. Plus, I didn't break promises even if they were disgusting.

"Nothing to worry about." I checked my reflection in the rearview mirror and gave myself a pep talk. "They're not here for you, Cecily Bloom. You can slip in under the radar, eat some sushi, listen to Slash's bullshit and be done with it."

While acting made me feel whole and I adored it, I'd never loved the crap that went with it. Being famous came at a high price. The loss of privacy was the worst. Not that I was all that famous, but if the new TV show went according to plan, the vultures would come crawling out of the woodwork.

"Smile and walk fast," I told myself as I got out of the truck. Lowering my chin, I walked like I was living in New York City—quickly and with purpose.

The flashes from the cameras were blinding. Two aggressive jerks with pornstaches blocked my entrance to the restaurant. I looked around to see who in the hell had shown up. No one had shown up. I found it very difficult to believe they were here for me.

"Cecily," someone yelled from behind me. "This way! Show us that beautiful smile, babe."

I was not his *babe*. But what I didn't want was to be on the front page of the tabloids with a surly expression. Keeping my eye roll in check, I turned and gave the turds what they wanted.

"Is it true that you and Slash are back together?" another leach shouted.

My smile felt brittle on my face. I was going to skin Slash alive when I made it into the restaurant. He'd obviously called the vultures with a tip on our fictional new relationship status.

"Nope," I said in a pleasant tone. "We're just old friends."

"Not what Slash said," another yelled and punctuated it with a lewd laugh.

Slash was so dead.

"Well, as you all *know*… Slash is prone to hallucinations," I said with a laugh so it wasn't clear if I was joking or serious.

The crowd went nuts. I was about to break out in hives.

"When's the new show airing?" Pornstache Number One yelled.

"January," I said with a real smile. "If you'll excuse me, gentlemen—and I use the term lightly—I have places to be and things to do."

"Like banging your ex?" an imbecile inquired with a suggestive smirk.

It made me wonder if he was a Demon. I squinted at him. Immortals glowed. Humans didn't. No glow. He was just an everyday asshole, not an Immortal one. I wanted to remove his head anyway, but revealing my own Demon status would ruin me.

Instead, I turned a homicidal glare on the man. "I'm sorry, what did you just say?" I asked icily.

The jerk backed away with an oily chuckle. However,

there was always another jerk in the tabloid cesspool to step up to the plate.

"Slash said you'll be doing the beast with two backs with him later tonight," Pornstache Number Two informed me with a wink.

Slash was going down. I shrugged and fake-winced. "Actually, that's impossible. Slash has erectile dysfunction. Hasn't been able to get it up for a decade."

"Holy shit," someone from the back bellowed. "Thanks for the scoop."

I smiled and waved. "Welcome."

Literally sprinting into the restaurant, I scanned the tables for the liar. The restaurant was packed. I spotted a few Oscar winners and an overabundance of reality stars. I hated scenes like this. They weren't my speed. The bar was on the back patio. My guess was that he was out there tying one on. Getting through the crowd was going to be tricky. Being pissed off, I didn't want to have to make polite chit-chat with anyone.

Handing Slash his ass then leaving was the plan. Doing the beast with two backs wasn't part of the deal. Where the hell was the asshole?

"Babe, your outfit would look great on my bedroom floor," Slash whispered in my ear from behind. He put his arms around me and ground his pitiful erection into my backside.

My elbow was a useful body part. I wound it up, threw it back hard and knocked the wind right out of him. If I'd been thinking clearly, I would have aimed lower.

"What did you tell the leaches out there?" I hissed.

Due to the fact that Slash was a washed-up rock star and I was currently known as a former child star, our conversation barely registered to the people nearby. We weren't cool enough and that suited me just fine.

My ex was doubled over and trying to catch his breath. "I told them the truth, babe. You and me forever. Didn't know you were into the rough stuff. Me likey."

"Me no likey," I snapped. "Let's get this straight right now. This is not a date. It's an obligation on my part. I do *not* want to sleep with you. Ever. It's not happening."

Slash stood up. The grin on his face was so wide I was tempted to slap it off. "Playing hard to get is hot, babe. With school, I always wanted to get an A. With you, I just wanna F."

"You're a pig."

"Are you a drill sergeant?" he asked with a smirk, pointing to the gross bulge in his pants. "Because you have my cock standing at attention."

"Let me help you with that," I said with a smile.

The idiot thought he'd won. He was incorrect.

Kneeing him in the nards wasn't my finest moment, but it felt fabulous. As the rock star writhed on the floor, I squatted down and got in his face.

"Slash, you're an asshole. I never should have married you all those decades ago. You have the maturity level of a fourth-grade boy. Your dick isn't big and you're not that great in the sack. If I never see your sorry ass again, it will be too soon. And if you ever insinuate that we're together to the press again, I will sue you and I will own you," I ground out, using my agent Cher's line to Abaddon from earlier today. It was a good one. "I'm going to the bar to have a drink. Alone. The dinner is over. Have a terrific life and thanks for the backstage passes."

As I made my way to the bar, I heard him yell that he'd call me. Braindead didn't even begin to describe him.

This had been one of the worst days of my life. One glass of merlot was needed to calm down. I was surprised I wasn't escorted out after I'd wracked a rock star, but this was LA. Everyone got wracked on the regular whether it be literal or metaphorical.

"That was badass, my liege," Fifi whispered in my ear as I made my way out of the dining area and outside to the bar.

I had to slap my hand over my mouth to keep from screaming. My self-proclaimed Succubus bodyguard had to stop sneaking up on me or I was going to have a nervous breakdown. Fifi was six feet tall with piercing green eyes and auburn hair. The woman was gorgeous with a resting bitch face that was terrifying. She was also fond of grenades and frequently offered to off my enemies by sucking the life force out of them during sex. I had not taken her up on that.

"What are you doing here?" I demanded. My heart raced as if I'd just run a marathon.

"Protecting you," she replied, looking crestfallen at the tone of my voice.

I put my hand on her shoulder. "Thank you, but as you can see, I can protect myself."

She nodded sheepishly. I felt awful. Fifi was a sweet gal in a psychotic, grenade-carrying way.

I sighed. After the altercation between my knee and

Slash's nuts, it was comforting to see a friend. "You wanna have a drink with me? My treat."

The Succubus smiled. "I would be most honored, my liege."

"Great," I said, steering us toward the bar. A horrible thought occurred. "Are you carrying grenades?"

"But of course, would you like one?" she asked as if we were speaking about something as mundane as the weather.

"Umm... no, and I don't want you using one here."

"No problem, my liege," she said with a small salute. "I'll use knives if necessary."

"Hopefully, it won't be necessary," I said with a sigh. It was a violent world I'd unwillingly entered and it didn't seem like there was any going back.

I paused our forward motion and looked at my crazy new friend. "Where did you stay last night?" She'd relocated from Vegas to LA to protect me... yesterday.

"Ophelia's," she told me with a shudder. "She's a very messy Demon and she snores. I'm looking into buying the house next door to yours."

"It's for sale?" I asked. I hadn't noticed a sign.

"No, but money talks," she said with a grin.

I inhaled and knew I'd probably live to regret what was about to come out of my mouth, but went for it anyway. "I have a guest room. You can stay there if you don't mind bunking with Uncle Joe. I'm not even sure if he sleeps."

"I'm very impressed with Uncle Joe. I've never been ambushed by ghostly testicles until today. It was brilliantly foul. I'm considering asking him to be my mentor. He's an adorable dead man, wrinkled ball sac and all. If he doesn't mind my presence, I would be delighted to take my liege up on the kind offer."

"I'm pretty sure he'll be fine with it, but we can ask when we get home."

My date was officially over, and I had a new housemate who made a damn good drinking buddy when she wasn't trying to blow shit to pieces. The night was finally looking up.

And that's, of course, when everything went terribly wrong.

The view from the outdoor bar was pristine white sand and the Pacific Ocean. There were a few tables scattered on the beach for the guests. They were all empty. Surprisingly, the bar wasn't crowded. Maybe it wasn't so surprising. A crowd had formed around Slash and emptied the patio area. However, it wasn't completely deserted.

My stalker was here with his gal pal by his side.

My skin felt hot and the flush quickly rose to my cheeks. The invasion of my privacy was one thing. The throwing of the new bang-buddy in my face was vicious. The bitchy Demon Shiva wore what I could only describe as a low-cut hooker dress. She was stunning even in the tasteless and tiny piece of material barely covering her body. She sipped seductively on a Bloody Mary. It was appropriate considering I wanted to head butt her—Bloody Shiva had a lovely ring to it. For the most part, Abaddon wasn't paying her much attention, but the message he was sending was crystal clear. He'd moved on in a nuclear option way.

"Unbelievable," I muttered under my breath. Having a

beer at home with Fifi, Sean and Man-mom was the new game plan.

"Would you like to sit with Abaddon or not?" Fifi asked.

"Not," I ground out, shoving my hands into the pockets of my dress because they were about to ignite.

The Succubus frowned. "I thought you knew he was here."

"You thought wrong."

Fifi tensed up. "Shall I shank them for you, my liege? It would give me great pleasure."

For an unhinged second, I almost said yes. My new tendency to jump right to violence was bad. I was losing myself. My lips compressed into a thin line. I now understood Abaddon's need to put his fist through a wall. Although, planting my fist in his face would be far more satisfying. Pressing the bridge of my nose, I swallowed back the need to sob. What the hell was happening to me? I wasn't a violent person... but I was fast becoming one. I'd lopped off a few heads recently, I'd stabbed Abaddon, and I'd wracked Slash.

Something Lilith had said came back to me—*Anger is healthy unless it consumes you.* I might not want a mother-daughter relationship with the woman, but her words were wise. Abaddon would not consume me. Uncle Joe had been correct, too. There was indeed a thin line between love and hate. I was now leaning hard into the hate camp.

"No shanking," I said. "But I'd rather chew broken glass than spend time with him. Let's get out of here."

"As you wish," she replied.

Exiting the way I'd arrived was impossible. The restaurant was crowded. Part of me was tempted to poof away, but that wasn't smart. Even though there weren't many people outside, there were some. While I was still unclear of the rules, it made sense not to freak humans out with magic.

"The beach," Fifi said. "We can go to the beach then around the building to the parking lot."

I nodded and started moving. From the corner of my eye, I noticed Abaddon rise to his feet and follow. Shiva pouted and tried to grab his arm. He shoved her away. The exchange was stupidly satisfying. However, the reality was that I was stupid—satisfied and seriously stupid. What they did or didn't do wasn't my business. I'd made that clear when I'd cast the spell and broken the compulsion Abaddon had on me. Sadly, it had only worked on him. Too bad, so sad. His disgusting behavior would kill any love I still had for him.

"Faster," I insisted, glad I'd worn flats. I had nothing to say to Abaddon and I didn't want to hear anything he had to say to me. At work, I'd deal with him. In life, I would not.

We hit the beach at a quick clip. I was relieved that Fifi hadn't thrown me over her shoulder like she'd done at the Golden Showers Bet and Bed. That would have been mortifying.

"Crap," I muttered as the ringtone for Man-mom blasted in my purse.

He knew where I was. My dad had no reason to call unless there was an emergency. My stomach tightened and I pulled Fifi to a stop.

"I have to get this. It's my dad," I told her as I spied

Abaddon catching up. "Keep him away from me, please. I'll deal with him after I talk to Man-mom."

"Your wish is my command, my liege," Fifi said, retrieving a grenade and a dagger from her jacket.

Pulling my phone out of my bag, I touched her arm. "Do not kill or maim him."

The Succubus looked disappointed, but nodded curtly before moving quickly to cut the Demon off.

"Dad?" I said, worried. "Are you okay?"

The voice on the other end of the line was not my father's. I felt dizzy and dropped to my knees in the sand. Fifi and Abaddon were in a physical altercation only ten feet away. I barely noticed.

"Who is this?" I ground out even though I recognized the voice.

She was supposed to be in time-out. Candy Vargo the toothpick-loving badass Keeper of Fate had promised me that Pandora wouldn't be my problem for ten years. My dad and brother were supposed to be safe.

"I'm your worst nightmare, Cecily Bloom," Pandora purred with a laugh so vile it made me sick.

"You're in time out," I snapped, hoping she was playing some kind of fucked-up trick on me by cloning my dad's phone number. "You won't be my nightmare for a decade."

Fifi had not been able to stop Abaddon. They were both bloody and banged up as they stood on either side of me.

"Your father is such a handsome man," Pandora said in a seductive tone, ignoring what I'd just said.

No. This wasn't happening. Not Man-mom. He was safe. I'd kept him safe. Hadn't I? My body shook violently. I dropped my phone. Abaddon picked it up and put it on speaker.

"I understand why Lilith was so taken with him. I think we'll have so much fun together," she purred over the tiny speaker.

Abaddon's eyes turned blood red with fury, but he didn't make a sound. He pointed at Fifi to stay quiet then squatted down next to me. He held the phone close enough for me to be heard when I spoke.

"You're a liar," I ground out.

"Thank you," she replied coldly. "Normally, yes, but not today."

My eyes filled with tears. I swiped them away with my forearm. She had to be lying.

"Prove it," I said, keeping my tone as even as I could when all I wanted to do was scream. "Let me talk to him."

"As you wish," she said with an unhinged laugh.

"Cecily?" my dad asked, sounding like he hadn't slept in weeks.

I dug my flaming hands into the sand so I didn't blow up the entirety of Malibu.

"Dad, it's me," I said shakily. "Are you okay?"

The question was absurd. He was obviously not okay.

"I'm okay, Cecily-boo. Don't come after me. That's what she wants."

Pandora's hysterical laughter in the background made my skin crawl.

Man-mom continued, sounding weaker with each word. "I'm an old man. I've lived a wonderful life. Remember when I told you I would step in front of a train to save you or Sean?"

"I do," I whispered as tears rolled down my cheeks.

"The train has arrived," he said softly. "I meant it then and I mean it now. I love you, Cecily-boo, and I always will."

I could hear the smile in his voice. It made me cry harder. How was this happening? How did the scum of the Universe break out of Demon jail?

"Wasn't that sweet?" Pandora snarled, back on the line. "Would you like to make a deal, *Cecily-boo?*"

My nickname on her lips was horrendous. "What are the terms?"

Abaddon shook his head. I put my hand up to let him know this was my problem and he wasn't involved.

"Your life for your father's," she said gleefully. "Even trade, little Goddess. No stress, no mess."

I sucked back my tears. I was a badass. Badasses took care of their own. "Where and when?"

"That's for me to know and you to figure out," she hissed. "And you'd better figure it out quick. Daddy Dearest has three days before he breathes no more. Good luck, Cecily-boo. You will need it."

The call went dead as my panic attack roared to life. My vision blurred and my head felt like it was going to explode. Getting air into my lungs was painful and difficult. My dad was one of the most precious people in my life. His love for me and mine for him was the most real and unconditional love I'd known.

The arms around me were strong and comforting. The

words whispered in my ear were calming. I rested my head on a strong chest. Slowly, my breathing became normal. Slowly, the pain in my head receded. Slowly, my vision cleared.

I knew who held me. It felt so incredibly right even though it was tragically wrong. God, how I wanted it to be different.

As soon as it was clear that I was okay, the Demon abruptly let me go and moved away. I felt the loss acutely. That was my problem. Not his. I'd get over it. I stood up and took a deep breath.

Maybe, Abaddon would help me. He'd had a longtime friendship with my father. He might despise me, but it was impossible to hate Bill Bloom.

I steeled myself to feel nothing and looked right into Abaddon's eyes. "I need your help."

Shiva's hiss of displeasure from behind him made me see red. Without thinking, I raised my hand and electrocuted the living daylights out of her. I was lucky no humans were around to witness it. Her furious shouts were enjoyable. I wiggled my fingers and doused the flames that covered her. I also dressed her in a burlap sack.

"I've had enough, Sheba. One more shitty word out of you and you'll be bald and sporting facial hair. I'm not encroaching on your territory. Your lover will be home to you soon."

Abaddon looked at me as if I'd lost my mind. I had, but not about this.

"I am not—" he started.

My hand shot up. The Demon had a lot more to say, evidenced by his incredulous expression. All I needed was the answer to my question. "Don't care and don't want to know. All I need to know is if you'll help me find my dad."

"You're an idiot, Cecily," he said.

"Correct. Is that your answer? Because if it is, I'll move on to someone else."

His eyes narrowed. "Thought you already did." His voice was flat, but his red eyes showed his ire.

I didn't have time for games. He was not the one for me, and I was not the one for him. It had been a mistake to ask for his help. I had Lilith's number memorized. I would call her. I knew in my heart she was as invested in my dad's safety as I was. And while she couldn't engage directly with Pandora since they were the two Demon Goddesses who lorded over the Darkness, I could.

And I would.

I glanced over at Fifi, who was holding a grenade in each hand, ready to lob it at Abaddon or Shiva. "We're out," I told her.

"No, you're not," Abaddon snapped, grabbing my hands and holding them in a vise-like grip. "I'll help you."

"Are you being honest?" I asked. "I can't have your hatred for me getting in the way of saving my dad."

The Demon was pissed. His eyes literally shot red sparks. "Again, you're an idiot."

"Already established," I said. "I need your word that you'll put aside your feelings and be loyal to me for the next few days."

He laughed. I didn't get the joke.

"You have my word, Goddess Cecily," he replied with the barest hint of a smile on his lips.

I nodded. "Fifi, let the others know what happened and make sure Sean is okay. Protect my brother with your life."

"On it," she replied, vanishing in a bright and glittery rose-colored mist.

"Shiva," I said, looking at the soaking-wet, burlap-covered Demon. "You will alert Lilith. Immediately."

"Yes, Goddess Cecily," she replied woodenly before she poofed away.

I didn't trust her, but Abaddon and Lilith did. I'd have to give a little.

"Are you ready?" Abaddon asked with an expression I couldn't decipher.

The question seemed loaded but I took it at face value. "Where are we going?"

His head tilted to the side, and he stared at my lips for a moment. "To the Darkness."

I closed my eyes and tried to find the serene feeling I'd experienced with Uncle Joe after our yoga session. It was nowhere to be found.

"Take me to Hell, Demon," I said.

His beauty was stupid. His smile held secrets. "If we go, there may be no coming back."

Again, I knew he was saying much more than his words implied. Again, it didn't matter. All that mattered was bringing Man-mom safely home. Period.

"Take me anyway," I said.

"*Nothing* would give me more pleasure."

In a blast of shimmering black magic, we left Malibu.

I had no clue what was coming next, but I'd cried my

river of tears and built a bridge to get over it. I would cross it as a badass and maybe even live to tell.

The train had not arrived to take my dad.

Pandora was not the train.

I was the train, and I was going to tie her to the tracks and run her over until she was unrecognizable even to herself.

Time to get the party started.

CHAPTER TWO

I GLANCED AROUND IN CONFUSION. THIS WASN'T THE Darkness, or if it was it looked like a small sleepy town somewhere down south. Weeping willows rustled in the wind and the scent of honeysuckle filled the air. We'd gone from mid-evening in LA to the middle of the night somewhere else if the moon was any indication.

"Umm... did you poof us to the wrong place? This doesn't look like Hell to me."

We were sitting in a minivan that wasn't mine and probably wasn't his either in front of a Piggly Wiggly supermarket. I couldn't picture Abaddon owning a minivan. It was absurd.

"Depends on your perspective of Hell," he replied, looking over at me and sizing up my outfit and sand filled hair. "That won't do."

I glared at him. At least I wasn't covered in dried blood like he was. My outfit was cute. He was a dick. With a wave of his hand, my dress was gone. In its place were jeans, a fitted long sleeve white t-shirt and black Doc Maarten boots. It was an outfit I would have chosen for myself, but I wasn't going to say thank you. Dick wasn't being nice. He was being practical. With another wave of his hand, his evening wear disappeared, and he was dressed similarly to me.

Sadly, it was hot.

Ignoring my randy lady bits, I pushed for answers. My dad's life was on the line, and I didn't have time for a joyride. "Why are we at a grocery store? Is Pandora food shopping?"

The Demon eyed me like I was insane. Considering where we were, I thought the question was logical.

"Pandora doesn't shop for her food," he replied flatly.

I took a deep breath so I didn't electrocute him. "Good to know. Do you happen to own the minivan we're currently sitting in?"

"I do not."

I couldn't help myself. I electrocuted Dick. He laughed. It barely affected the Demon. I was done. If he wasn't going to help me, I was out of here. I'd poofed by myself once. I could do it again. If I could get myself back to my house in California, I would powwow with Cher, Fifi and Ophelia. After that, I'd call Lilith. Shiva would have already let her know what was happening. Fifi, Cher and Ophelia had my back because they were my friends. Lilith had my back because she was my egg donor. It was also clear that she still had deep feelings for Man-mom.

I wanted to electrocute myself for thinking I could trust

Abaddon. Going to Lilith and my friends should have been my first plan.

"Don't do it, Cecily," Abaddon warned.

I was going to be seriously pissed if the asshat could read my mind. "Do what?"

"Leave. It's not wise."

I raised my middle finger. Ophelia had not been a good influence on me. However, the rude gesture felt great. "I need to find where Pandora is holding my dad. I don't need to buy chips and a soda, Dick."

Abaddon was emotionless. "And how do you propose doing that?"

"Poof back home. Grab a few grenades from Fifi. Get Cher's opinion. Bribe Ophelia to be my second then call Lilith for help," I shot back.

Abaddon pressed his lips together. I wasn't sure if he was furious or trying not to laugh. Erring on the side of caution, I electrocuted him again. Again, he laughed.

Completely ignoring that I'd just set him on fire, he calmly doused the flames then shot down my plan point by point. "Fifi's grenades will not kill Demons—they'll simply piss them off. There's also the chance you could harm your father with a grenade. Cher is an Angel, not a Demon—big difference. Her input is irrelevant. While Ophelia is loyal, she's also a loose cannon. Her hatred for Pandora could cause you problems. As far as calling Lilith in at the start, I'd advise against it."

I closed my eyes and willed myself to stay calm. He made sense… mostly.

"Explain Ophelia's hatred of Pandora."

Abaddon shrugged. "Not my story to tell."

Blowing out a frustrated sigh, I kept going. "Why is bringing Lilith in immediately a bad idea?"

The Demon leveled me with a hard gaze. "The Goddess will have to be brought in eventually. She's already been alerted by Shiva, but she'll proceed with caution unless her hand is forced. She loves Bill in a very real way. Her judgment will be clouded. It could mean the end for more than just your father."

I took in what he said. He was a gazillion years older than me and had far more experience. His coldness bothered me, but I listened. Letting my emotions get the best of me would not help Man-mom. Methodical, logical and deadly precise action was necessary.

For my dad, I would do anything—even get along and work side by side with Abaddon. I wished to the Darkness and back not to have feelings for the horrible man. It would've been much easier if I felt nothing. My taste in men had never been a strong point of mine. Abaddon was just another jerk in the long list of jerks I'd have to get over. Hopefully, sooner rather than later.

I nodded curtly. "Tell me why we're at the Piggly Wiggly. And is it open at this time of night?"

"It's open twenty-four hours, seven days a week. Candy Vargo works here. She has some explaining to do," he ground out as his eyes turned a sparkling blood red.

I was surprised that Candy worked at the Piggly Wiggly. However, she was an odd one.

Abaddon needed to tamp the red eyes back if we were about to be around humans. A joke was in order. "Don't you mean, Candy has some 'splainin' to do, Ricky Ricardo?"

The joke didn't land. The Demon had no clue about TV or pop culture. He'd obviously never seen *I Love Lucy*. Whatever. I'd tried.

"Forget that," I said, pointing to his eyes. "You look like a Demon."

"I am a Demon," he replied.

"Right. You want to advertise it?"

The gorgeous jackass closed his eyes for a brief moment. When he opened them, they were normal. It was a neat trick.

"We're going to need to talk at some point, Cecily," he said. "Are you ready to go into the store?"

I was not. I wasn't ready for any of what was happening, but that didn't matter. My dad was in danger. It didn't matter that I didn't want to be a Demon. It was irrelevant that my mother had popped back into my life after forty years. Other than her helping me save my dad, I wanted nothing to do with her. That ship had sailed. No one cared that I was hung up on a man who had been under a compulsion to love me until I broke the spell. It was neither here nor there that I was going to be looking over my shoulder for what appeared to be a very long life.

The idea that none of this would be happening if I conveniently died was at the forefront of my mind. Trading my life for my dad's was beginning to seem like a no-brainer. Man-mom would be devastated, but he and my brother would be safe. Finding out from the Keeper of Fate how Pandora escaped her time-out was key.

Right now, knowledge might be more powerful than magic.

"I'm ready."

～

WHAT THE HELL?" I MUTTERED, PULLING ABADDON TO A STOP at the entrance of the store. Touching him made my hand tingle. I yanked it back as if I'd touched fire.

He gave me a glance and a raised brow full of obnoxious innuendo then scanned the Piggly Wiggly. The mostly empty establishment felt hostile and dangerous. The low growl from deep in Abaddon's throat didn't help my frayed nerves. The interior of the grocery store wasn't out of the ordinary. The aisles looked like any other random grocery. It was the occupants inside who were unexpected.

I knew every single one of them.

They stared at me with curiosity, and from the looks of it, derision. However, they were unsettled by Abaddon's presence. No big surprise there. Forget the fact the man was a Demon, there was no way they could know that. The scowl on his face was terrifying. As much as I hadn't wanted to ask him for help, I was happy he was by my side. Even though he was an asshole, he calmed me like no one else ever had.

"Where are we?" I asked quietly.

He squinted at me. "The Piggly Wiggly."

"No duh," I snapped. "What state?"

"Georgia," he replied.

Now the scene in front of me made even less sense.

Candy Vargo stood behind the register. There were no other cashiers but her. Her arms were crossed over her chest and she was glowing dangerously. Six people—all of whom I was familiar with—were lined up to pay for their purchases. They were the only people in the store along with the angry Keeper of Fate and us. Candy wasn't having it. She stared daggers at the gathering of customers.

A few looked uncomfortable, the others were as calm as cucumbers. They were idiots. Candy Vargo was known to eat people who pissed her off.

Eyeing the line warily, I began to tick them off in my head.

Stella Stevens was first in line holding a package of breakfast cereal. Time had not been her friend. The over-abundance of plastic surgery had been cut rate—the actress looked like she'd gotten stuck in a wind tunnel. She was a five-foot nothing waste of space who'd put itching powder down my pants right before what could have been a life-changing callback for a super hero movie at a major studio. It had been years ago, but I was still living that one down. I didn't get the part, but rumors had spread all over Holly-wood that I had the crabs. Suffice it to say, I didn't like Stella Stevens.

Next in line was Corny Crackers. He gripped a box of douche in his gnarled hands like it was a winning lottery ticket. I never wanted to know in this lifetime why he was buying douche. Shockingly, Corny Crackers was the name the old and very negative geezer had been born with. He carried around his birth certificate to prove it. I would have ended my parents if they'd named me Corny Crackers. I'd done a movie of the week with him. He'd played my dad. Off camera, he'd hit on me repeatedly. It was disgusting. Twice I'd been treated to the visual of his wrinkled junk. To get the old man to back off, I had my dresser steal his dentures. I refused to give them back until I had it in writing that he'd sexually harassed me and would never bother me again. He knew I'd go straight to the tabloids if I had to which would ruin his nice guy persona. It was before the Me-Too movement, when jackasses like Corny didn't see anything wrong with exposing their ding-dongs to women on the regular. The pilfering of the dentures was genius. The idiot didn't want the world to know he was toothless. I'd dipped them in the toilet before returning them. It was the little things that created the most joy.

The movie we'd done had stunk. My character, Miranda Diamond, had moved back home from the big city to help with the failing family Christmas tree business called the Bush Bonanza. The matriarch of the family had passed on in a bizarre gardening accident that was referred to constantly but never explained. That was bad, but it got worse. Much to my own personal horror—not Miranda's—I'd given up my swanky, high-paying job in NYC, came home and fell in love with a lumberjack/ horticulturist who didn't speak English. Dolph Gunter—played by a guy whose name I couldn't recall. No one could explain the oxymoron of his jobs… He was supposed to be German but sounded more like The Swedish Chef from the Muppets. He'd also had some seriously bad breath and there had been far too many kissing scenes. I'd refused to watch it when it aired.

Sean and Man-mom had thought it was hilarious. It wasn't a comedy.

Behind Corny Crackers stood Jonny Jones. Jonny was super handsome and lacking in the brains department. If I remembered correctly, he'd been fond of the words, babe, guy and 'in my opinion.' His *opinions* left everyone open mouthed in confusion. He'd been a mostly pleasant guy who I'd done an informercial with for a knock-off version of Transformers. Instead of the robot turning into a cool car, it was a possessed-looking doll that turned into a flowerpot. It had been taken off the market when customers complained that the crotch of the demonic doll was too anatomically correct. I'd had nightmares about that job for months. However, the gig had paid great.

Jonny Jones held a baby doll and a box of diapers in his hands. The doll wasn't as whacked-looking as the one from the informercial, but it wasn't great. Then again, Piggly Wiggly was a grocery store—not a toy store. What did I expect?

I almost rolled my eyes as I noted the next in line— Moon Sunny Swartz. There weren't a whole lot of good things to say about Moon. She was basically un-hirable in Hollywood. The certifiable gal was known for playing pranks on set. Last I'd heard, she had nine restraining orders against her. My agent had repped her for one day then kicked her to the curb after Moon had put a poisonous snake in Cher's office toilet. I'd done a TV pilot with the whacko eleven-ish years ago called *Roommates*. Basically, it was a ripped-off version of *Friends*. Moon had been caught in a *prank* getting jiggy with the furniture on the set during

31

lunch break. The couch hadn't survived. Unfortunately, the debasement of the furniture had been on the same day the studio heads were watching the show. She'd recorded her performance and put it on the internet. It had gone viral. The show didn't get picked up. It hadn't been that great of a sitcom, but Moon humping the armchairs, and everything else in sight, had been the nail in the coffin for that production.

Moon Sunny Swartz held a can of furniture polish in her hands. The irony was too much.

What I didn't expect was the next person in the line. I had no clue what her name was since I'd referred to her as Obnoxious Ponytail Girl back in the day. She was competitive, mean and flexible.

"What the actual fuck?" I muttered under my breath.

If I'd ever known her name, I'd blocked it out. The last time I'd seen her was at the callback for the kids show *Lou's News* where I'd concussed myself and knocked out a few of my teeth. Sadly, there weren't enough scouring pads in the world to scrub that painful callback from my memories since I still had a scar on my face and a few implants in my mouth as a reminder. Needless to say, I didn't book the job. Neither did she.

That had been twenty years ago. The nasty piece of work still sported a ponytail and was more obnoxious than she was then if the unattractive smirk on her enhanced fish-lips was anything to go by. I half expected her to do a cartwheel and slide into the splits. Obnoxious Ponytail Girl had a basket full of heating pads, ice packs and joint pain cream.

I smiled. Those cartwheels had caught up with her.

What I still didn't understand was why they were in a Piggly Wiggly in Georgia. However, it was the last person in line who alarmed me the most.

An old and decrepit woman stood at the end of the line. I'd never worked with her, but I knew her at a bone deep level. The woman was in disguise. She made eye contact, raised a gray brow and gave the slightest shake of her head. I wasn't going to have to ask my mother for help. She was already here.

I spared a quick glance at Abaddon to see if he recognized her. If he did, he wasn't letting on.

Everyone stared at me and waited. For what? I had no clue. Nothing about the situation made sense. A half hour ago I'd been in LA. I'd poofed to Georgia with Abaddon into a what seemed to be a combative standoff with a bunch of random people from my past... in a Piggly Wiggly. Peculiar and creepy were the words that came to mind. I stared at Candy Vargo for a long moment. She was glowing and looked like she was about to implode.

Wait a freaking minute.

Something was way off, besides the fact that the worst of the worst people I'd worked with were in a Piggly Wiggly in Georgia. Candy Vargo wouldn't glow in front of humans. From what I'd been told we had to keep the voodoo under wraps.

Immortals glowed. Humans did not. I squinted my eyes and stared at the line of people.

"Shit," I whispered. Apparently, I'd worked with a lot of people who were older than dirt in my career.

"What?" Abaddon asked without moving his lips.

"They're all Immortal."

He nodded tersely. "Demons."

The utter strangeness of this didn't bode well. I felt it in my gut.

"Bout time you fuckers got here," Candy Vargo griped, chewing on a toothpick. "These asshats scared all the human customers out of my damn store."

"What are you all doing here?" I demanded, narrowing my eyes at the group. I included my mother in my glare. She wasn't aggressive at all, but I didn't want to blow her cover.

Candy grunted. "Fine fuckin' question. But then again, there's a butt for every toilet seat."

I almost laughed. Candy Vargo was a piece of work, but I liked her. She thought of me as a badass and I was doing my best to live up to her assessment.

Corny Crackers stepped forward. I instinctively took a step back. The man was abhorrent.

"We have your contract, Cecily Bloom," he said with a leer that made my skin crawl and caused Abaddon to growl.

"For?" I asked.

"The reality show," Moon Sunny Swartz chimed in with a thumbs up.

"Confused," I stated flatly. "I don't do reality TV."

"You do now," Obnoxious Ponytail Girl announced with a vile grin as she sauntered on over.

Abaddon moved to stop her, but I touched his arm to hold him back. It seemed clear that these Demons—other than my mother—wanted a piece of me. Showing any weakness was a huge no-no.

I no longer needed to get angry to call on my purple fire

sword. Granted, Obnoxious Ponytail Girl—henceforth known as PT Bitch—definitely pissed me off, but that was neither here nor there. With a quick wave of my hand, I produced my weapon.

PT Bitch stopped dead in her tracks. Her eyes went wide and she quickly looked over her shoulder to see if she was alone in her stupidity of advancing on me.

She was.

"I'm going to need a bit more information," I said calmly. "Step back into the line, PT Bitch."

Her eyes flashed red and she hissed. "What did you just call me?"

"My apologies," I said with a smile that didn't reach my eyes. "I meant Obnoxious Ponytail Girl."

"I have a name," she snapped.

"Congrats," I replied. "Info now, or we can fight. Your call, kids."

I eyed the unnerved group and heard Abaddon chuckle softly.

Candy Vargo cackled at full volume. "My girl is a fuckin' badass," she warned the Demons. "You don't wanna mess with her. Heard it through the grapevine she eats people."

I suppressed a gag with enormous effort. The Keeper of Fate was incorrect, but the expressions of horror on the faces of Stella Stevens, Corny Crackers, Jonny Jones, Moon Sunny Swartz and PT Bitch kept me from correcting the nutty woman.

Only the Goddess Lilith in her old woman disguise cracked a small smile. It was clear that the actors and actresses—and I used those terms lightly—had no clue that there was a goddess in their midst. I was still unsure if Candy and Abaddon were clued in.

Jonny Jones gave me his lady-killer smile and wink. "So, babe, in my opinion," he began.

I sucked some air in through my teeth and ignored Abaddon's grunt of displeasure. He had no say over me. He was banging Shiva. However, I had rights and dumb-dumb Jonny Jones wasn't going to step on them.

"Let me stop you right there, Jonny." My tone was flat. Retracting my sword, I glared at the idiot. "My name isn't babe. It's Cecily. If you insist on calling me babe, I'll have to electrocute you. We clear?"

"Fuck that," Candy yelled, clearly enjoying herself. "She'll eat you and not in the good way."

I held up my hand to the Keeper of Fate. While I appreciated her confidence in me, puking wouldn't help my case with the Demons here to challenge me.

Corny Crackers held out the sheaf of papers and shook it impatiently. "It's all in the contract."

"All of Cecily's contracts go through her agent," Abaddon informed him coldly as his eyes blazed red.

Old Corny tamped back his impatience quickly. Abaddon could be a very scary Demon.

"Correct. My agent handles all my contracts." I didn't have time for this shit. Man-mom needed me. Now.

"Not this one," Stella Stevens stated. Her face barely moved. She'd obviously overdone the Botox.

"Sign it," Moon insisted. "The show starts tomorrow night. If you don't sign, we all die."

I rolled my eyes. A game was being played that I didn't

understand and from the looks of it, neither did Abaddon, my mother or Candy Vargo.

"This is givin' me gas," Candy Vargo shouted, lifting her leg and letting one rip in the direction of the *customers*.

As the line of Immortals tried to run from the appalling stench, Candy waved her hand and dropped an enchanted iron cage around the crew. Lilith wasn't trapped inside with the others. It was now clear that my mother's disguise didn't fool Candy. It didn't fool Abaddon either. With a gag, he quickly stepped forward and moved the old woman out of the waft of stinky.

The others were trapped in the cage and choking. PT Bitch threw up. I was grateful that I wasn't down wind of Candy's evil butt weapon.

"Umm... Candy was that necessary?" I asked, pinching my nose.

"Better out than in," she replied with a wicked grin. "And unless those assholes start talkin', I'm thinkin' I might have to cut the cheese again."

Stella Stevens screamed like she was dying. Corny Crackers frantically douched his nose. PT Bitch dry heaved in the corner of the cage. Moon aimed her ass at Candy and tried to return fire. That didn't go according to plan. Candy chuckled and created a wind that turned Moon Sunny Swartz around. Moon's airborne toxic event hit her cohorts. PT Bitch punched the prankster in the head so violently, it wouldn't have surprised me if she'd knocked it off. Jonny Jones staggered around the cage then passed out.

I'd never witnessed anything like it in my life. It was gross. It was funny. It was weird. It was rank. The Keeper of

Fate's methods would have made a pack of second grade boys proud. While I'd never borrow that particular page from her book, I was impressed that no one had died. Knowing how vicious Candy Vargo could be, this move—while disgusting—was actually mild.

The Goddess in disguise covertly waved her hand and removed the stench. No one in the cage witnessed the magic. They barely acknowledged her presence. It wasn't clear if they knew she was here. Candy eyeballed my mother with annoyance, but Lilith simply ignored her.

"I'll talk," Stella Stevens shrieked. "I'll tell you anything you want to know as long as that woman doesn't flatulate again."

Candy reached under the counter and produced a can of beans. She ripped the metal lid off with her teeth, sat down on the conveyor belt and began to eat with her fingers. The Keeper of Fate's entire body sparkled ominously. Her warning was clear. Her words were even clearer.

"You with the frozen fuckin' face," she said, pointing at Stella with bean juice covered fingers. "First, nobody tells me what to do. Ever. Second, if you don't come clean and answer Cecily's questions, my next tushy cough is gonna happen while I'm sittin' on your nose. Ain't no one can survive that. Third, ease up on the Botox. My bowels move more than your face."

I closed my eyes and bit down on my lips so I didn't laugh. The entire situation was so awful it was funny. I supposed the saving grace was that she hadn't eaten them.

Yet.

It was time to figure out what was going on. It appeared

increasingly obvious as of late that not much in the Immortal world happened without reason.

"What's the reality show?" I asked, keeping my distance from the cage just in case Candy ripped another.

From the floor Jonny Jones came to and piped up. "It's called *Demivor Running Man Games*."

No one added anything to the unusual title.

Candy belched. "Next time, that's coming out of my ass."

All the Immortals in the cage began talking at once. It was unintelligible. Abaddon was over it. He raised his hands and electrocuted the living daylights out of all five.

"One at a time," he ground out through clenched teeth. "You first." He pointed at Corny Crackers.

The idiot gripped his douche in one hand and the contract in the other. His hair was on fire, but he didn't notice. "It's a combination of *The Hunger Games*, *Running Man* and *Survivor*—played exclusively by Demons. Hence, *Demivor Running Man Games*."

The Demons needed better marketing people. The title of the show, while horrifying in reality, was stupid.

Lilith paled and walked away down the condiment aisle. That wasn't a great sign. However, the fact that she was here meant something large was at play. It seemed it was up to me to suss out the information.

"Where's the show being shot?" I asked.

"In the desert outside of Vegas," Moon answered.

"Of course, it is," I muttered. "Who are the players?"

"Us and you," Stella said, referring to the asphyxiated crew.

"Let me get this straight," Abaddon snapped in a voice so

filled with raw fury all the occupants of the cage backed themselves into the corner. "The six of you shall fight to the death?"

"Yes," Jonny Jones said. "In my opinion it's rather mundane and predictable. Would be much more exciting if it were a baking contest or even a dance off. The judges could just decapitate the one with the worst snickerdoodles or the most ungraceful tango. Much more civil. An added plus would be if we all spoke in British accents."

I was immediately reminded of Jonny's lack of brain matter.

"How many fuckin' times did your momma drop you on your head as a baby?" Candy asked, shaking her head in bewilderment.

Jonny was confused. "None that I know of."

"Alrighty then," Candy said. "Here's the deal. If you say anything else stupid, I'll drop you on your head."

"Could you define stupid?" Jonny asked, giving her his thousand-watt smile.

She rolled her eyes, removed the cage with a snap of her fingers, and walked over to Jonny. He was still gracing her with his smile. I winced preemptively. Candy didn't disappoint. She picked up the grinning fool like he weighed no more than a feather and dropped him on his head.

"You have anything else to add, motherfucker?" she inquired.

Jonny Jones shook his bruised head. Candy nodded curtly and went back to the conveyor belt.

"Jonny Jones is incorrect as to how the game is played," PT Bitch snapped.

"No surprise there," Moon said.

It was the first time since I'd known Moon Sunny Swartz that I agreed with her.

"Speak," Abaddon ground out furiously.

The five stared at each other then pushed PT Bitch forward.

"Screw all of you," she hissed at her cohorts.

"It can be arranged, babe," Jonny Jones assured her with his over-the-top smile.

PT Bitch marched over to him, did a repeat of Candy Vargo's head drop move then set him on fire. Moon, not wanting to be left out of anything violent, beat the flames out as if he'd attacked her first. It was awful. I felt kind of sorry for Jonny Jones.

Abaddon was fuming. His power saturated the room and it became difficult to breathe. Candy Vargo had bent over and was ready to *cut the cheese* again.

Corny Crackers gasped in horror then quickly stepped over the moaning Jonny Jones and took over. "We're not supposed to kill each other during the game," he began.

"Speak for yourself," Stella muttered. "I'd enjoy offing all of you."

Moon Sunny Swartz was on a roll. She headbutted Stella then gut punched her. "Do not interrupt," she snarled at the now bleeding Stella.

Corny cleared his throat and continued as if people maiming each other was the norm. "The six of us will be let loose in a staged Vegas town in the desert. We're permitted to form alliances—like *The Hunger Games*. We must survive twenty-four hours—not exact, but similar to

Survivor. And we will be running from assassins—like *Running Man*."

It didn't sound like a show I wanted any part of. It was psycho.

"The program will be live streamed on the Demon Network," Moon announced, looking excited about the shitshow.

"What if more than one is alive at the end of twenty-four hours?" I asked, beginning to think this was connected to my father somehow and there was likely no getting out of it.

"If there's more than one, they will go head-to-head in a death match," PT Bitch said with a gleeful expression.

"Absolutely not," Abaddon snapped.

I shot him a look and shook my head. He wasn't being asked to play the game. I was. I needed more information before I declined the *job*. "What's the prize for the winner?"

"It's lame," PT Bitch griped.

"Quite," Corny Crackers agreed.

The hair on my arms stood up and a chill skittered up my spine. I had a feeling that our definitions of lame differed greatly. "Not what I asked."

"A human man is the prize," Moon Sunny Swartz said with a shrug. "Kinda shitty, but I need the work."

I heard Lilith gasp. Abaddon swore. I felt like I was going to puke, but now I was fairly sure I understood the game.

"Who's producing the show?" I questioned.

"Pandora," PT Bitch said sounding bored.

The only person who was shocked at the answer was Candy Vargo. She detonated the cash register. I moved quickly to her before she blew up the Piggly Wiggly. "I've got this."

She eyed me long and hard then shrugged.

I walked over to Corny Crackers and held my hand out for the contract. "Give it to me."

He handed it over. Moon tossed me a pen. "You going to sign that without reading it?"

I glared at her. She smiled. All the others stepped back in fear. The woman had a death wish.

"What's the name of the human man?" I demanded.

"Bill something or other," PT Bitch confirmed what I'd already suspected.

Pandora was dangling my father as a prize hoping I wouldn't survive the game. Her filthy hands would stay clean if she didn't technically end me. It was devious and smart. She'd lied on the phone, but that wasn't a surprise. To win I was going to have to dodge assassins then possibly eliminate, in a permanent way, a person I knew. I was about to play a game where there were no winners in the end. The thought made me sick. Pandora was beyond evil.

Abaddon made his displeasure known by demolishing several aisles of the store. After he'd destroyed the baking aisle, he pulled his shit back together and rejoined the motley crew of Immortals assembled. They had all paled considerably. While I would've liked to have joined him in blowing up inanimate objects, I didn't. The game wasn't his to play. It was mine.

And I was going to play it for my dad.

I signed the contract. I didn't need to read it. What it said was irrelevant. My father's life was on the line. I was smart enough to understand there was no negotiating. I was going to do my best to win without killing anyone who wasn't trying to kill me. I didn't like Moon, Jonny, Stella, Corny or PT Bitch, but I didn't want them dead.

"Ballsy," Stella Stevens said.

"Badass," Candy Vargo corrected her right before she put her fist through the wall and knocked down a huge display of chips and tin foil.

"Answer me this." I addressed the group. "I know why I'm playing this game. Why are you?"

All refused to answer. While not surprising, it was frustrating. I could tell by his stance and his irate glare that Abaddon wanted to torture it out of them. That wouldn't help anything.

I knew there was far more than met the eye. Plus, Demons lied. That was a fact.

"Where outside of Vegas is the show being shot? Is there an address?"

Corny Crackers smiled. It wasn't pretty. He tossed me a copy of the contract I'd signed. "It's all there in black and white. See you tomorrow, Cecily Bloom."

In a gust of red mist, Corny Crackers, Stella Stevens, Jonny Jones, Moon Sunny Swartz and PT Bitch disappeared.

I turned to Candy Vargo. "You have some explaining to do."

She tossed me a box of toothpicks as she waved her hand and cleaned up the store. I caught them and put one in my mouth.

"I'd suggest somewhere a little more fuckin' private," she said.

"Fine by me. Where?"

"My house," she replied.

If her house was anything like her, I was going to need a shower afterwards.

CHAPTER THREE

HOUSE WAS AN UNDERSTATEMENT. IT WAS A MANSION IN THE middle of nowhere. Candy had insisted on taking her car. I knew that as a Demon I was difficult to kill, but Candy Vargo's driving was terrifying. I was certain we weren't going to live through it. The worst was when she raced over a train track with an oncoming train. She laughed like an unhinged loon when the back of her car got clipped. Abaddon and Lilith were strangely calm. I screamed. Candy called me a pussy and I flipped her off.

She loved that. Note to self… never get in a car with Candy Vargo again.

"You inherited the Archangel Michael's home?" Lilith asked as we stood in a massive and ornate foyer.

I had no clue who the Archangel Michael was, but he must have been loaded. The home was mostly white and marble—kind of on the cold side. However, there were children's bikes, art supplies, baby dolls and sports equipment all over the place. I recalled the Keeper of Fate saying she had foster kids. As bizarre as she was, the woman clearly had a soft spot for children.

"Daisy gave it to me," Candy said looking around at the formal home with an amused expression. "Not my fuckin' style, but I got a gaggle of youngins and need the space."

Abaddon was silent. He held the contract in his hands and looked it over. His expression was unreadable. Lilith, no longer in disguise, walked over to a white couch and seated herself. My eyes were drawn to my mother's ethereal beauty. I forced myself to look away. Pretty outer shells didn't mean the insides matched. I scolded my inner child who had longed for her. That was then. This was now. That ship had sailed.

Pressing my clenched fists to my sides so I didn't punch a wall, I marveled that no one seemed overly concerned. Everyone's calm demeanor was freaking me out. Was I the only one who cared that Pandora had kidnapped my dad?

I felt incredibly alone even though I wasn't.

The *job,* for lack of a better term, that I'd signed on for was potentially the kind that permanently rearranged one's heart and sense of stability. Although, the word stability wasn't in my vocabulary anymore. Barely contained chaos was how I would describe my present state of mind.

Two of the occupants in the foyer could have meant something to me if the Universe was a different and kinder place. I'd wanted a mother my entire life. Now that she was here, I felt very little but anger for the woman. Granted, since we'd met, she'd been fair and on my side, but it wasn't enough. My fury was something I needed to deal with in therapy. She was so damned selfish to have seduced my dad and created me. I was the piece of the vicious puzzle that upended a world I hadn't known existed until recently. My existence was what had made Pandora kidnap my dad. My demise would right the natural order.

Ignorance was indeed bliss. I wished I could go back. It wasn't possible.

And Abaddon... even looking at him made my heart hammer in my chest and my head hurt. My life as I'd known it for forty years had ended when I'd learned I was a Demon. Believing had taken some convincing. Abaddon had convinced me, and when he had, I'd tumbled off the love cliff and into his arms. I'd made plenty of mistakes in my life, but this one came in first place. The humiliation of learning he'd been compelled to love me was too much. I was half human and I wasn't buying into that this was how Demons did it. It was bullshit... and sad.

So, I did what I'd had to do. I'd used my newfound power to break the compulsion and give the Demon back his free will. He'd accepted his freedom after he'd blown up a building then upped the ante by banging his former gal pal.

Whatever. It simply proved my point. However, it didn't feel good. Being near him was ripping me apart from the inside out. If it hadn't been for my dad, I'd have run like a pack of flaming Demon assholes were trying to remove my head.

Too bad, so sad.

Candy Vargo, as uncouth as she was, was the only person I felt semi-comfortable with at the moment. She didn't hide who she was. She lived her life in an openly disgusting way. I was all for it.

Speaking of being open… The Immortals I'd come across so far had been cryptic. It was annoying as all get out.

"Can we get down to business?" I asked tersely as I paced back and forth. "How did Pandora escape her time-out?"

"I've got no fuckin' idea," Candy grunted. "Someone opened the box."

I was lost. "She was put in a box?"

"Metaphorically and somewhat literally speaking, yes. Every motherfucker creates their own Hell even if they're unaware of it. For some it's greed. For some asshats it's excess. For others it's something tangible. Only fuckin' narcissists create a tactile Hell. It's the height of ego to expose how to destroy a being," Candy said, kicking a soccer ball into a crystal chandelier. It came crashing to the ground and scattered all over the place.

Abaddon and my mother were on me like white on rice to make sure I wasn't shredded by the jagged crystal. I rolled my eyes and walked away from both of them. In the past few days, I'd defeated crap a lot more dangerous than freaking shards of crystal.

Leaning against a pristine white wall that was at least three stories high, I examined the trio. Trying to be dispassionate was difficult. Emotions would get me in trouble. My goal was clear. Save my dad. These people could help me. It was immaterial how I felt about them.

Candy Vargo wanted nothing from me as far as I knew. She'd backed me up in front of other Immortals when I had no other ally. In my book that made me like her. I assumed she liked me too, but I would be an idiot to assume. I'd made an ass out of myself far too often lately. She had a gift that could help me. I was going to test her friendship shortly.

I held that thought.

The next person my eyes landed on was my mother... or egg donor to be more specific. Lilith was one of the two goddesses of the Darkness along with Pandora. I was very aware she couldn't have a go at Pandora. There was something in the Demon Laws—which was an oxymoron in itself since they were a violent and lawless crowd—that forbid the two in charge from physically challenging each other. Unfortunately, I was a Demon goddess as well. My birthright made it so. It threw off the balance and that could mean the end of everything. My mother was more powerful with me on her side. Pandora didn't like that. Honestly, I didn't blame her. Even though I hated the vile woman, I understood her deranged dilemma.

I needed to beat Pandora at her game, rescue my dad and put her nasty ass back in her box, so to speak. It was a tall order, but the risk of losing my dad was unacceptable. I'd willingly give up my career, my fortune and every other material thing in my life to win. Hell, I was prepared to give up my life. My mind raced. My thoughts were scattered. A bird flew in through the open front door and circled the foyer before flying back out. The position of the bird, Candy, Abaddon, Lilith and myself made me have an absurd déjà vu. A terrible movie I'd done pushed itself to the fore-front of my brain.

I'd played an amnesia victim named Myrtle in a shitty B

movie years ago where I'd been terrorized by my mother...
but she wasn't my mother at all. She was the scorned
woman who'd loved my deadbeat dad and stolen me from
the hospital before my real mom could get to me. The
nutjob had lost her mind because my dad didn't love her.
For a year I'd endured her abuse until one day I *miraculously*
recalled everything after a pigeon had taken a dump on my
head. My avian buddy and I had become fast friends. I'd
sent a note with the homing pigeon to my real mother with
a plan I'd hatched while scrubbing the bathroom floor of
the whacko who'd abducted me.

Even thinking about the plot made me wince in embar-
rassment. My old agent, not Cher, had convinced me I'd
win an Emmy. She'd been sorely mistaken. I didn't work for
two years after that shitshow had come out. I'd fired her.

It was called *You're Not My Damn Mother*. The title was
as bad as the movie. When my real mother had shown up,
the batshit crazy kidnapper tried to kill her. I'd pretended
not to know my mother until the cops and my deadbeat
dad arrived on the scene. I'd convinced that nightmare of a
woman I was on her side with some seriously bad acting—
including tears and snot. In the moment, it had felt great.
When I watched it on playback, I'd wanted to die...
violently. Of course, the movie had a real "Hollywood"
ending... The whack job got arrested after she'd lost her
shit and monologed every bad thing she'd done in her life
to the police officers. My mom and dad fell back in love in
the five short minutes it took the cops to drag the freak
out from under the kitchen table and into the back of the
cop car... and we all lived happily ever after with our new

pet and hero of the shitty movie, our homing pigeon, Steve.

Of all the freaking things that could have popped into my mind, I couldn't believe it was *You're Not My Damn Mother*. I shook my head and smiled. While the movie had been a disaster, my real life eclipsed it. Where was a homing pigeon when you needed one?

"Somethin' funny, motherfucker?" Candy Vargo asked.

"Painfully," I muttered.

All three stared at me in confusion. I wasn't about to enlighten them. I focused on Candy. "When you said Pandora was let out of a metaphorical and somewhat literal box, what did you mean?"

The Keeper of Fate shot my mom a loaded look. Lilith held her gaze and said nothing. Abaddon looked like he wanted to kill something.

None of this was working for me. If they weren't talking, so be it. Going it alone wasn't my preference, but a gal with a kidnapped father did what she had to do. I walked over to Abaddon and held out my hand. "Give me the contract."

His eyes blazed red, and his jaw was clenched. "It's bullshit, and I'd advise against it." It was clear he was doing his damnedest not to blow up Candy's fancy abode. The man needed some anger management courses.

"Not your choice to make," I replied coolly. I read the first page of the five-page document. Page one alone was enough to make me want to hurl. I put the offensive papers down on a marble table covered in crystal shards. I'd read it later. It didn't matter what it said. I was doing it. However, it would be smart to get familiar with the fine print. I

turned my attention away from Abaddon and back to
Candy. It was time to test our friendship. "You're the Keeper
of Fate. What's my fate?"

She chuckled and pulled a toothpick from her pocket.
"Not the way it works, badass."

"Enlighten me."

She eyed me for a long moment then tossed me a box of
toothpicks covered in gold foil. "Do not lose those. They're
good for pickin' things if you know what I mean."

I tucked them into my pocket and waited. Hopefully, it
would be more useful than a box of toothpicks.

She didn't leave me hanging. "What's more powerful
than evil?"

I shrugged. "Decapitation?"

From the corner of my eye, I spotted my mother wince.
Abaddon simply closed his eyes and pressed his temples.

Candy chuckled. "I like your style, girlie."

While the reactions of my mother and former almost
lover made me lose some confidence, I soldiered on. There
wasn't much choice. If they weren't going to offer help, I
was going it on my own. "Did I get it right?"

"Hell no," Candy replied with a grunt of laughter. "Try
again, badass."

"Electrocution?" I guessed. Candy was a violent gal. I
figured the answer had to be bloody.

"Nope," she said.

I hesitated before my next guess. But when in Rome…
"Cannibalism?"

"Jesus H. Christ," Candy snapped. "Enough with eating
motherfuckers. While I'm all for administering appro-

priate pest control, you need to go in a different direction."

I groaned. Normally, I loved the guessing game. Tonight? Not so much.

Different direction? I could do that. I had until eight PM tomorrow night before the *Demivor Running Man Games* started according to page one of the contract. It was around three in the morning now in Georgia. Granted the time change in Vegas was screwing me up a little, I was going to make it work. There wasn't much of a choice.

"Define fate," I demanded of my toothpick loving ally.

Candy Vargo grinned. I took that as a good sign. I kept my gaze on her and didn't let it stray to either Abaddon or Lilith. Candy believed me to be a badass. I needed her confidence in me to help boost my own.

"Fate's a fickle fucker," she began as she grabbed a chair upholstered in white silk and straddled it. "Some of that shit can't be determined by the decisions that an individual makes."

"Like when a person is born? That's set in stone?" I asked, pulling up my own chair and straddling it just like my uncouth friend had. It felt unladylike and awesome.

"Bingo," she stated. "There are other things that fate has a hand in too."

"Like?" I asked.

She raised a brow and crossed her arms over her chest. "You gonna throw a fit if you don't like the answer?"

"Is that a trick question?" I shot back.

"Depends," she replied. "Some would swear that your other half was fated."

I rolled my eyes. This wasn't necessary. What I wanted and needed was help with saving Man-mom from Pandora's evil clutches. Candy's words made me nauseous. I had more than enough on my plate. Worrying that I'd f-ed up my life by breaking the compulsion that Abaddon was under to love me wasn't something I could deal with. Plus, I stood by my own words that I wanted someone to love me because they wanted to... not because they had to. Period.

"You're forgetting about free will and destiny," I countered coolly.

"Am I?" she questioned.

"You are," I assured her as I heard Abaddon make a rude noise. I didn't grace the asshole with a glance.

Well, now," Candy continued moving on from her last statement. "Destiny is an entirely other beast. It's about the present. Every single decision you make leads you to your present scenario."

Wrinkling my nose, I tried to understand how any of what she'd said applied. However, the definition wasn't volunteered. I'd asked. It might not apply at all. "Destiny is malleable and fate's not?"

"Not that simple," Candy explained. "Faith is stronger than destiny."

"Well, shit," I muttered. I wasn't a real religious person. And I was now seriously confused. "Faith in a higher being?"

She shrugged. "Can be. Doesn't have to be. Faith in self or someone else, as long as the intention is good, works."

I nodded then ran my hands through my hair in frustration. "Am I asking the wrong questions?"

"Ain't no such thing as a wrong question, badass. Knowledge is power," Candy assured me. "But you've gotten a little off track."

I stared hard at her and willed her to lay it all out. She didn't but she gave me a way in.

"You have to earn your information in the Immortal world," she said.

I rolled my eyes. "Fine. How?"

Candy grinned and picked her ear with her toothpick. I seriously hoped that toothpick didn't make its way back into her mouth. "Well, if I'm rememberin' right, you like that quote game."

I squinted at the woman in surprise. I'd only met her recently. How did she know that?

The Keeper of Fate winked at me. It made me smile. I wasn't sure why, but it felt right. She had said she'd kept track of me over the years. It must've included spying on me if she knew the silly games Man-mom, Sean and I'd played.

"You remember your kickass fuckin' karate teacher way back when you were in elementary school?"

Now I was certain she'd spied on me and most likely my dad and brother too. And yes, I recalled my karate teacher. Her name was Coco Margo and she showed up every Thursday at four PM sharp for years. She was insane and Sean and I had adored her. Not only had I learned to defend myself and break a board, but the crazy woman had taught me and my brother every swear word known to man. We'd kept that nifty fact a secret from Man-mom because we didn't want Coco to get fired. I still had the yellow notebook where I'd kept a list of the profanities taught to us by our whackadoo and hilarious karate teacher. Sean and I had to look a lot of them up. Even now, when we needed a good laugh, we'd snack on a few jazz cabbage gummies and I'd pull out that tattered notebook and recite the filthy words to my brother. Coco stuck by Sean and me for six years. We were both black belts by the time she retired. The woman was like a crazy aunt with a mouth like a sailor. She was also fond of... toothpicks.

"What the...?" My eyes narrowed to slits as I glared at Candy Vargo and tried not to laugh. It wasn't possible to be mad at her. She'd been a true highlight of my childhood. It was abundantly clear she'd used the alias Coco Margo—made sense, Coco was candy and Margo rhymed with Vargo. The two looked nothing alike, but I knew Immortals could disguise themselves. There was a very good reason I felt so comfortable with Candy Vargo. I knew her, or a version of her. I'd adored her then and now.

She threw her head back and cackled. "Sneaky, huh?"

I joined her. I laughed and shook my head. "Very. And thanks to your shitty vocabulary, I got my mouth washed out by our prissy tutor on the set of *Camp Bites*."

"Sorry, not sorry, motherfucker," she said with a wide grin. "So, here's the deal. You get the quote right and I give you a cryptic hint."

"How about you give me a straightforward hint instead?" I suggested.

"No can do," she said. "Rules are rules. You gotta be the master of your own damn destiny. Shit sticks a whole lot better when you have to figure it out instead of being spoon fed like a baby."

Abaddon and Lilith were quiet. That was fine. Candy was my main girl. I wouldn't give a hoot if they left.

"I'll play… Coco Margo," I told her.

"The evil you do stays with you. The good you do returns to you," she quoted.

"Buddha also known as Gautama or Siddhartha," I replied with a wink of my own.

"Correct," she said, tossing the earwax covered toothpick to the ground and pulling out a clean one.

I was wildly relieved she did that. It would be impossible to stop myself from yanking the dirty one out of her mouth. Since she was attached to her pieces of wood and was extremely violent, that could have been a bad move on my part.

"Spit out a cryptic hint," I told her. "We have a deal."

She pointed her toothpick at me. "Metaphorical doesn't mean it's not real."

I committed the words to memory. It seemed like she was referring to Pandora's box, but with Candy one could never be sure.

Candy continued. "Good can exist without evil, whereas evil cannot exist without good."

Again, I knew the quoter. "Saint Thomas Aquinas."

"Bingo, badass," she said, impressed. "Here's a nice cryptic message to chew on… nothing in this world is more powerful than dread necessity."

That one made sense. "Got it," I replied. I felt that one in my gut. Hopefully, it meant I was up to the task of saving my dad. It would be nice to come out of the shitshow alive, but I was willing to die.

"Try this one on for size," she challenged with a raised brow. "Tell me who said, 'I believe that unarmed truth and unconditional love will have the final word in reality. This is why right, temporarily defeated, is stronger than evil triumphant'?"

"Martin Luther King Jr," I said without missing a beat. I realized the quotes she chose were as important as the cryptic hints. I listened carefully to all of it. The Immortals were a mystery, but I was beginning to understand the way they worked… a little bit. It was like running in a never-ending circle—no beginning and no end.

"Smart cookie." She gave me a thumbs up with one hand and the middle finger with the other.

From anyone else, it would be rude. From Candy Vargo it was a show of affection. I gave her the middle finger salute back. She grinned so wide it had to have hurt her cheeks.

"Just because you don't understand something doesn't mean it's not fuckin' true." She punctuated the oblique statement with a double middle finger birdie gesture.

I was pretty sure the foul signal meant the hint was important. There was a hell of a lot I didn't understand about being a Demon. More than anything, I wished I wasn't a Demon. If wishes were horses beggars would ride.

"Want to be more specific?" I questioned.

"Nope."

It was the answer I'd expected. But one could always try.

Candy wasn't done with the game. "A soulmate is someone to whom we feel profoundly connected, as though the communication and communing that takes place between us were not the product of intentional efforts, but rather a divine grace."

Abaddon sucked in an audible breath. This was moving into uncomfortable territory. I knew who the quote was attributed to. It was one I'd repeated to myself over the years when I'd wished for someone special in my life. I was tempted to blow the answer to get out of the game, but knowledge was power and I needed all I could get.

Ignoring the intense stare of Abaddon that I could feel even though my gaze was on Candy Vargo, I answered her. "Thomas Moore."

"Yep. Now tell me what's stronger than evil?" she demanded.

I sighed. She'd basically banged me over the head with it. "Love. Love can defeat evil."

"Ding, ding, ding, motherfucker," she sang as she stood up and took a bow. The Keeper of Fate then eyed Lilith. "You wanna add to this conversation?"

"When the time is right, yes," she replied.

The time felt pretty right to me, but I knew that pushing wasn't going to work. The people I was dealing with were older than dirt and nuts.

"So, I just have to survive the assassins and love Pandora?" I asked sarcastically.

"For a badass, you're a dumbass," Candy stated as she stood up and yawned. "I'm gonna hit the sack. Got a big day tomorrow."

My mouth fell open. I couldn't believe she was serious. "But I need you."

The Keeper of Fate walked over to me and kissed my cheek. "I don't like people. They suck."

Candy looked me in the eye as she spoke. I wasn't real sure where she was going, but I hoped it didn't end in bloodshed.

"But I like you, badass. Loved you since you were an obnoxious little squirt. Also have a soft spot for your brother. I'll tell you one more thing... there are many ways to box someone in. In order to capture, one might want to captivate. You understand?"

"Umm... no."

She laughed. "You will. I believe in you, motherfucker. Pull from what you know and wing the rest of it. Love you, badass."

"I love you too," I whispered.

"Yep, I'm pretty fuckin' lovable," she said with a chuckle. "So, all that shit bein' said, if I had more for you, I'd give it to you. I ain't a Demon. I'm just a plain old Immortal who works at the Piggly Wiggly and collects foster kids who need me."

She was not just a plain Immortal. She was a beautiful, disgusting, powerful Immortal who I really did love.

"Thank you, Candy," I told her as I leaned in and hugged her. "I'll prove my badass-dom to you."

"Damn right you will." She patted my pocket that held the toothpicks. "Wood might not be metal, but in a pinch, it works just as good."

I had no clue what she meant, but knew it was probably important.

"Got it."

"And now you need to make peace with your own," she said, giving me the eyeball.

I wrinkled my nose and sighed. I was aware she was referring to Lilith and Abaddon. "They're not mine."

The Keeper of Fate rolled her eyes. "Did you listen to a fuckin' word I said this evening?"

"I did."

"Then be the badass," she said. "Be. The. Badass."

With a wave of her hand, Candy Vargo disappeared in a blast of shimmering orange magic. I wasn't sure if she transported herself to wherever her bedroom was or if she'd really left. It didn't matter. She'd made her point abundantly clear.

I would be the badass.

CHAPTER FOUR

I WAS UNSURE HOW TO PROCEED. TIME WAS TICKING, SO I DID the only thing I could think of to do. I walked back over to the table and picked up the contract.

It would have been great to be able to rely on a mom who happened to be a Demon Goddess or a partner who loved me, but that was a fantasy. I was all about reality right now as bizarre and unsettling as it was. Candy said they were my people. It didn't feel that way. Hostile and cold was how I would describe it.

Or maybe I was the hostile and cold one. Whatever. I had no idea how to *make nice* with my people. It didn't help that I didn't want to be one of my people… My mother and I couldn't replace forty missed years in a few hours. And I was pretty sure there was no undoing the spell I'd cast on Abaddon to give him back his free will so he wasn't forced to want me. I was batting a whole lot of zeros. My luck needed to change fast.

Both of the Demons in the foyer looked eager to speak. Lilith's expression was filled with compassion and love. It cut like a knife. I reminded myself that I was forty, not five. Abaddon's face was unreadable and made me feel breathless. Not good. Looking at him made me have to acknowledge what I'd ruined. I held up my hand to stop them. Contract first. Chat after.

Neither Lilith nor Abaddon said a word as I read. I could feel Abaddon's intensity. The air in the room grew heavy with it. Sitting down was necessary so I didn't pass out from the magic wafting around.

I took shallow breaths and read some more.

The contract was bad. Abaddon had been right in his assessment of what I was getting into. However, I wasn't backing down. I couldn't. Letting Pandora be the train my dad stepped in front of for me wasn't going to happen. I didn't want to give negative thoughts any power, but there was a good chance I might not survive. Honestly, I was fine with that. It solved a host of issues for people I loved, mainly my dad and brother. As long as Man-mom survived, I was good. Heck, I'd just come back as a ghost and hang out with dead Uncle Joe. Although, I'd wear clothes.

The rules of the game were absurd and dangerous. Not a big surprise considering the source.

I wasn't allowed any outside help or I'd forfeit the game and would be put to death.

We were encouraged to pick an ally, but if our ally died by the hand of the assassins, we would have to forfeit our life as well.

There would be cameras all over the fake town that had

been set up in the desert outside of Vegas. It would be broadcast to Demons on their special network. That was bad for so many reasons. If there were some who didn't know about my heritage yet, they would soon. It was unclear if the assassins had access to the footage. Since Pandora was producing—for lack of a shittier phrase like setting us all up for death—it probably meant they could. Hunting us would be easier that way.

I rescanned the offensive papers to see if I'd missed anything about that.

I hadn't.

The prize was the human man named Bill Bloom. My heart sunk as I looked at my dad's name in black and white. The lifeless print on the paper didn't capture the beauty of my dad. Bill Jackson Bloom was a distracted man of profound wisdom. He was absent minded and funny. He gave the best hugs in the Universe. Bill Jackson Bloom was absurdly handsome and created questionably weird works of art. His clothes were always splattered with paint. His smile lit up a room. He'd single handedly raised me and Sean with love and lots of peanut butter and jelly sandwiches. He was my hero.

Swiping at the tears in my eyes, I read on. Bill Bloom would be handed over to the winner by Pandora when the last player was still standing. If all of the contestants died, the human would be returned to his home.

I didn't believe that for a second. She was a lying piece of vile shit. Although, from what I'd experienced so far, Demons weren't permitted to harm humans.

The other good part was that Pandora would be present

when I won. And I would. But I needed to know a few more things before I started the job.

Slowly, I turned and faced *my own*. "Does the box exist?" Lilith paled and nodded. "It does, Cecily."

My name on her lips made me feel whole, but I didn't let on. Emotions would weaken me. I was ready to break as it was. Adding to my heartache wasn't smart. "Where is it?" I demanded.

My mother shook her head. "It's not the box you want. Any number of boxes would work. It's the key that you need."

I closed my eyes and wanted to peel my skin off my body. Instead, I stayed calm. Kind of… My hands were sparking, and I was pretty sure my purple fire sword was about to pop out. "Do you know where the key is?"

The Goddess Lilith's eyes blazed red. "If I did, I would hand it over. Pandora has taken the key to my personal Hell by abducting my soulmate and demanding you trade your life for his. I can't go on without him… or you."

"You could have fooled me," I said flatly. "You've been AWOL for forty years. Doesn't sound like you give a damn."

"You know nothing," she whispered.

"And whose fault is that?" I ground out. My heart beat so rapidly in my chest, I was sure I was about to have a heart attack.

Lilith looked down at her tightly clasped hands. After a long agonizing moment, she spoke. "Mine. The fault is mine."

"You're the one who put my father at risk with your self-ishness. You're the one who gave birth to the spawn who could end the world as we know it, whatever that even means. When I save my father, I'll end Pandora. And I *will* save my father no thanks to you."

"Killing Pandora will solve nothing. It will bring on complete chaos," Lilith said.

I glared at her as a thought occurred to me. I needed more information. "The farked up model that you Demons have is that there must be two Goddesses of the Darkness?"

Lilith grew uncomfortable under my gaze. A huge part of me wanted to hug her and feel her arms around me. That was insane. I was insane. "That's the model. Yes."

I shrugged and laughed. It was humorless. "Fine. I'll kill the evil bitch and I'll become the second Goddess of the Darkness."

Abaddon walked over to the wall and punched it with such force, most of it came crumbling down. I held my breath and waited for Candy Vargo to come back and kick his ass.

It didn't happen. He very obviously didn't like my plan.

"There's a balance," Abaddon finally said with his back to me. "The two of you cannot rule together."

"I call bullshit," I snapped. I knew he hated me for what I'd done, but if he wasn't going to be helpful, he needed to leave.

"You can call whatever you want," he said as he turned and pinned me with an irate gaze. "The balance is between good and evil. Lilith is good. Pandora is evil. Both are needed for stability in the Darkness. Existence isn't black or white. It's gray."

Well, that certainly posed a problem. As much as I didn't

want to admit it, my mother was good. I had many faults, but being evil wasn't one of them.

Lilith stood up. Her power was as evident as Abaddon's, but it wasn't filled with rage. "This is not the place to discuss anything." She held out her hand to me. "Come with me, Cecily."

"Where?"

"I have safehouses on this plane," she explained. "As much as Candy Vargo can be trusted, we're not protected here."

"Which house?" Abaddon questioned warily.

"The main house," she replied in a tone that forbid him from disagreeing.

The Demon wasn't happy. He growled. It was terrifying. I was confused. Part of me leaned toward Abaddon and wanted to say no to the safehouse. However, Lilith had been around since the beginning of time for a reason. If she didn't feel that Candy Vargo's home was safe, I knew I should listen.

Reaching into my pocket to find a quarter to flip, which was ridiculous since the clothes I wore weren't mine, I smiled when my hand touched the gold foil box of tooth-picks Candy told me not to lose. Examining the package, I rolled my eyes. Etched in ruby red on one side of the box was the word *motherfucker*. On the other was *asshat*.

Motherfucker... I go to the safe house.

Asshat... I don't.

I tossed the box into the air much to the confusion of my mother and Abaddon. Motherfucker landed up. Safehouse it was.

I glanced around at the white marble palace littered with toys and sighed. Besides the fact that motherfucker had won out, Lilith had a point. There was a fine chance I was being hunted already. Pandora wanted me eliminated. How it was done was irrelevant.

I put my hand into the woman's who bore me. "Fine. Let's go to your safehouse."

POOFING WAS A BIZARRE MODE OF TRANSPORTATION. WHEN I'd done it by myself, it felt like I'd gone through a painful time warp. Luckily, my mother had much more finesse in the poofing-arena, which had made it less stomach churning. That was good. Puking in front of her and Abaddon would have been mortifying.

The safehouse was utterly charming in every way. The moonlight was bright and bathed the house in a glow that made it look enchanted.

I could feel both Lilith and Abaddon staring at me. I ignored it.

The cottage was nestled in the grass and trees as if it had grown up from the earth like nature. It conjured up all my childhood dreams of what a happy home should look like. It wasn't too big or too small. Flowering trees and expertly trimmed rose bushes surrounded the house. The exterior was a mix of gray fieldstone and white clapboard with a thatched roof and a deep red door.

Words danced in my mind as my eyes took in every single feature and memorized them... home is where the heart is… the difference between a house and a home is love.

I shook my head to get rid of the absurd thoughts. This was a safehouse. It belonged to Demons. It wasn't a home and it certainly wasn't my home.

"Where are we?" I questioned.

"At the safehouse," my mother answered hesitantly. She sounded nervous.

Her tone made my hackles rise. Lilith was one of the two Demon Goddesses of the Darkness. Hearing her sound unsure wasn't helpful. Why she would be anxious was beyond me. I had a big deadly game to play tomorrow. Playing games now wasn't in the plan.

I leveled her with a hard gaze. "I meant what state? Or country?"

Lilith inhaled deeply and nodded. "Oh, right. We're in California. Near Napa Valley."

I found it interesting that she had a house in California, but didn't comment. It wasn't exactly close to where I lived. The drive from LA to Napa was about eight hours. I wanted to ask if she spent much time here, but again, stayed silent. The thought that she could have been so close but hadn't reached out made me feel small and stupid.

Didn't matter. It was done. Living in the past was a waste of time. The goal was to live into the future.

The safehouse would provide protection until I had to be in Fake Vegas for the shitshow. I certainly didn't want to die before I had the chance to save my dad and deal with Pandora. The silence around me was loud in the quiet night. Abaddon was expressionless. It was heartbreaking that he'd

gone back to the cold man I'd first met. I was aware I was
the cause of his demeanor. Again, it didn't matter. Lilith, on
the other hand, looked like a child on Christmas morning.
The analogy was odd considering she was a Demon, but I
didn't know how else to describe it. I simply felt unsettled.

"Are we going to stand outside or go in?" I asked, rudely.
The longer we stood in uncomfortable silence, the more apt
I was to say or do something really dumb. My desire to hug
the woman who had deserted me forty years ago was
intense. I refused to go there. There was too much to
unpack and I didn't have the energy for it.

Crossing my fingers, I hoped she kept food in the safehouse. Eating then calling Cher, Ophelia and Fifi to check
on Sean was my plan.

"In," Lilith said, tentatively extending her hand for me to
go first.

As I approached the door, Abaddon appeared at my side.
I almost screamed. He'd moved fast and without a sound.
Being aware of my surroundings wasn't my strength. I
needed to work on that.

"Be kind to her," he said under his breath.

I squinted at him. "Be kind to who?"

"Your mother," he replied, whispering.

I rolled my eyes. "She's hardly my mother," I hissed as
quietly as he'd spoken.

The red door opened before we reached it. Dagon exited
the cottage. His eyes widened in surprise for a fleeting
moment when he spotted me. I was starting to feel really
wonky. Why in the hell did I trust a box of toothpicks to
decide if I was coming here? I should have stayed at Candy

Vargo's big white mansion. The Keeper of Fate was an open book. These people were full of secrets.

Dagon bowed his head in respect then graced me with a warm smile. I knew him. We'd fought together along with other Demons when we saved Abaddon from Pandora. I liked him. He was one of the few who was kind immediately. However, he was loyal to Lilith, not me. I kept that in mind as I extended my hand in greeting. Handshaking was a very human move. Dagon had been confused by it the first time I'd offered. Demons were formal. I wasn't. Refusing to let go of my human side, I stayed true to myself.

He gave me a wide grin as he shook my hand. "Welcome, Cecily. It's an honor to receive you here."

I raised a brow. Everyone was behaving so strangely, I half wondered if I was about to bite it. "You sure about that, Dagon?"

"Most definitely," he promised me.

Shiva stepped out of the house and stood with Dagon. The bitchy woman was as surprised to see me as Dagon was. She had a much harder time hiding it than he did. Her eyes narrowed angrily before she pulled her shit together and gave me a tight nod of respect. My instinct was to head-butt her, but I tamped it back. Jealousy was an ugly trait. Normally, I had a very good handle on my green-eyed monster, but Shiva brought it out of me in a big way.

It wasn't my business if she and Abaddon were doing the nasty. I'd taken myself out of the equation when I'd cast the spell and given the Demon back his free will. It smarted a bit that he'd gotten back into the game so quickly, but they were not my monkeys and their affair wasn't my circus.

Lying to myself that Abaddon and Shiva together didn't eat at my soul wasn't the easiest thing to do, but I figured if I repeated it in my mind enough, I'd eventually believe it.

Lilith placed her hand on my lower back and guided me into the cottage. No one followed. Dagon closed the door behind us after we entered.

Immediately turning on Lilith, I stood nose to nose with her. The house was dark and smelled like cookies. The desire to stay here forever was strong. Had some kind of spell been cast on me? Were Lilith and Abaddon trying to stop me from going after Pandora somehow? That would backfire on them. "What's going on?" I demanded. "Why are you and your people behaving so oddly?"

Lilith didn't say a word. She waved her hands and the cottage lit up. A warm golden glow revealed the interior. I glanced around and felt ill. It was a gut punch I hadn't expected. My eyes welled up with tears and I wanted to scream.

"Is this a sick joke?" I ground out.

"Not a joke, Cecily." She walked into the open and airy living room and sat down on a cozy green velvet couch.

I couldn't look at her. My eyes raked the scene. If she wanted to destroy me, she'd succeeded. Man-mom's art was everywhere—on the walls and tables. The paintings were lit professionally and painstakingly. It infuriated me that she owned the pieces my dad had created. However, it was the other *décor* that undid me.

It was so unfair.

Photos of me were all over the place—baby pictures, publicity photos, stills from films and TV shows. The cottage was a screwed-up shrine to Man-mom and me. There were images of me from every stage of my forty years. If she thought this would make me love her or feel sorry for her, she was wrong.

Dizziness overcame me. I squatted down and put my head in my hands. My breath came in short spurts of anger. The room felt claustrophobic and I wanted to leave. The toothpicks had betrayed me. Candy Vargo had told me not to lose them, but I wanted to set them on fire. It was wildly convenient to blame a box of wood for my decision to come here, but rational thought wasn't in my wheelhouse right now.

"This is fucked up," I muttered, staring at the floor.

Her hand on my back felt wonderful, but I jerked away as if she was a hornet's nest. "Don't," I snapped, moving to the far side of the room. "I'm not sure what you wanted to accomplish by bringing me here."

Lilith looked broken. She pressed the bridge of her nose and inhaled deeply. "Can I tell you a story?"

I laughed. It was hollow and mean. "Sure. Why not? You clearly live in a fantasy world. A story would be fascinating."

"Join me?" she asked, pointing to the couch.

"I'd rather not," I replied, holding onto my composure by a thread. She'd obviously watched me my entire life while I'd longed for her with everything I had. Part of me was thrilled that she'd obviously cared, but a bigger part of me wanted to punish her for it. I wanted her to feel the pain I'd felt.

She walked back over to the sofa and sat down. She clasped and unclasped her hands then placed them awkwardly on her lap. For a Goddess, she looked powerless. I got no satisfaction from her discomfort, and it was clear she got no pleasure from mine.

"When you live forever, it's easy to lose your humanity," she began slowly, searching for the right words. "I will not defend what I did because there's no defense. However, I don't regret it."

She paused as if she wanted me to speak. She was shit out of luck. The entire situation was abnormal and outlandish, but my feelings of resentment were very real.

"The compulsion to love for a Demon isn't nefarious," Lilith continued as my stomach tightened. "It's simply a way for someone who has very little hope of happiness to recognize the one who completes them."

Again, she paused. My skin felt clammy and I wanted to be anywhere other than where I was. I'd searched for answers my entire life and now I wasn't sure I wanted them.

"A soulmate connection isn't always sexual in nature," she explained. "Sometimes it is. For me it was. And even though it was incredibly selfish, I took it. It was the most precious time of my very long life. The year I had with your father was the only time I've ever felt true happiness. Your birth completed me in ways that would be difficult for you to understand."

My lips compressed and I fought back the urge to say something awful. My pain of abandonment was forefront in my brain. What might feel good in the moment wasn't going to serve me in the long run. I had the choice to listen to her story. I needed to hear it. For a second, I considered flipping the box of toothpicks again to make my decision. I refrained. At forty, I could make the selection without a childish game.

"Keep talking, Lilith," I said, trying not to cry.

"I won't apologize for loving Bill... for still loving him. I won't apologize for loving you either." She swiped a tear from her eye and kept talking. "What I am sorry for is that I wasn't able to be there for you."

"Or him," I added in a harsh tone.

She nodded and ran her hands through her dark curls—the same curly locks I'd inherited from her. "Or him," she conceded with sorrow. "I've done what I had to do to protect you. My greed to find a sliver of joy has put a deadly bounty on your head that you don't deserve."

If she was looking for compassion, I didn't have it to give. "Why did you choose to have me? Why did you go through with it knowing I would eventually be hunted like an animal?"

Lilith blanched and paled. The truth hurt.

"You were created in love... something that was so foreign to me and so very beautiful. Giving birth to you was my greatest joy and my most heartbreaking regret. I've stayed away to let you live. I didn't know you would be found."

My heart felt like it had risen to my mouth. Everything she said cut me to the core. She loved me. She regretted me. This sucked. I stared at the woman who had lived with her regrets and would live with them forever. My need to comfort her almost outweighed my good sense. Self-preservation was what saved me. I was close to breaking. There was no time for that. Man-mom needed me and I needed him.

Candy Vargo's cryptic hints and words were forefront in my mind. *Just because you don't understand something doesn't mean it's not true.*

There was a lot I didn't understand. Inside my human brain, it didn't compute. I'd been witness to the viciousness and debauchery of the Demons. It was horrible. Being part of their world had not been my choice. The utter scale of my life and what it now encompassed was difficult to fathom. Of course, the part about how Demons recognize their soulmate was particularly nauseating. I'd been a loser in love as a human and had torpedoed my chance at love as a Demon as well. My incompetence in the relationship department was mind-boggling. However, that was something I'd deal with another time... or never.

Steeling myself to hold back from going to Lilith, I blew out an audible breath. I understood love. I loved my dad. I loved my brother. I loved my friends. I still loved Abaddon who I'd royally messed up with. I wanted to love my mother, but it was too complicated to just dive in and pretend all the pain and hurt didn't exist.

"It's alarming and strange to be here," I admitted. "It's also confusing. I've spent my life wishing you loved me and hadn't left. Granted, there's a whole bunch of extraneous shit that I didn't know about... like the Demon part, but all I feel right now is anger."

Lilith's shoulders sagged and she gave me a sad smile. "I understand."

"No, you don't," I replied. I wasn't angry. My words were

simply my truth. "You can't because I don't understand. The fact that you have a home filled with inanimate objects that remind you of my dad and me is sweet and tragic. I suppose I'm glad to know that you didn't have a choice to stay... and that you loved us."

"Still love," she corrected me.

I didn't acknowledge that admission. "Fifteen minutes in a shrine that guts me isn't going to turn everything around," I told her. "I'm sorry."

Lilith stood up and wrapped her arms around her slim body. "I've missed the boat of being your mother," she stated in a matter-of-fact tone. "But I'd like a chance to truly know you and become your friend."

Weird didn't begin to describe the emotions that rioted through me. I bit down on my lips so I didn't let the hurt child inside me escape. I was an adult. The woman who bore me had no choice in leaving me if I was to stay alive. The Immortal world was a violent and unforgiving place. While I didn't want any part of it, that was fantasy. My life... this life... was fated to me. There was no changing who or what I was. However, destiny was mine to choose.

If I was honest with myself, which I normally thought was overrated, I liked the idea of getting to know Lilith. It was anyone's guess if I'd be able to accept her as my mother, but I could try to accept her as a friend. Man-mom had always told Sean and me that the truth was a lot easier to remember than lies. So, the truth it would be.

"I can work with that," I told Lilith. "I can't guarantee that it will succeed, but I'll give it a chance."

Her smile lit the room, and a delicate and ethereal magic

danced in the air. Lilith, the Goddess of the Darkness was a breathtaking woman. Her joy was contagious. I smiled against my will.

"May I hug you?" she asked warily.

I sighed. She was moving a little fast. "We can shake hands," I said, giving her a less intimate option. "We can work up to the hugs."

"Of course," she said, moving across the room with such speed she disappeared for a second.

She thrust out her hand with a loving grin on her lips. I took it in mine and squeezed. This was all kinds of nuts, but what in my life wasn't lately?

"Can you help me prepare to save Bill?" I asked as I continued to squeeze her hand.

"Yes," she replied. "And the others here will help as well."

Not loving the sound of that, I nodded anyway. I didn't like Shiva. She despised me. Abaddon was in the 'I hate Cecily camp' as well. Now that I knew what I knew, I didn't blame him. Only Dagon was a true ally. However, beggars couldn't be choosers. If Lilith believed the trio could aid me in saving my dad and bringing Pandora to justice, then so be it.

I was playing to win.

CHAPTER FIVE

When Lilith and I exited the cottage, I felt a huge sense of relief. As much as the shrine was sadly touching, it was too much. Focus was needed and I couldn't concentrate looking at the proof of her regret. Plus, I wasn't all that keen on seeing myself from every phase of my life so far.

"I'd suggest we go to the training area," Dagon announced.

I glanced around. All I spotted was a quaint cottage in the middle of nowhere. Abaddon noticed my confusion.

"It's behind the safehouse," he supplied, watching me carefully.

I didn't spare him a glance. It was too hard. What I'd done to us was FUBAR. Maybe with time we could be friends. And… maybe not. I'd granted his wish to be kind to Lilith. That was all I could give.

"I know how to fight," I stated. I was hoping for clues about how to bring down Pandora. The Grim Reaper, who happened to be my newly discovered uncle, had given me the gift to control my power. The fact that the Grim Reaper and uncle went in the same sentence was nuts. When in Crazy Town, one just needed to buy property and figure it out.

My magic was massive and frightened me, but right now I was grateful for every bit of it. I was going to need it.

Shiva sneered at me. I rolled my eyes. She was an idiot if she wanted to test the theory. She'd already seen me in action. No, I wasn't as old as the people here or the people I was about to play the game with, but as Candy said, nothing in this world is more powerful than dread necessity. I definitely had that going for me.

"You've been in one battle," Shiva pointed out rudely. "I've been in thousands."

"Congrats," I replied in a monotone. "Yay for you."

Shiva swore under her breath. Dagon didn't try to hide his amusement. Lilith watched the exchange with interest. I wasn't sure why she liked and trusted Shiva so much, but it wasn't my place to point out that the woman was a skanky bitch. And honestly, I could use the release of a smackdown. My nerves were frayed.

"I'd suggest one-on-ones with each of us," Dagon went on as if there was no extra tension in the air.

"Not smart," Abaddon said flatly, giving Shiva the stink eye.

The female Demon didn't like that. She lowered her chin and shot him a provocative glance filled with obscene promise. He ignored it. I winked at her. My bitchiness was showing.

"I'm fine with it," I said, disagreeing with Abaddon. "As long as decapitation is off the table, a few lessons are a fine idea."

"Decapitation is *off* the table," Lilith stated harshly as she looked over and addressed Shiva. "If you believe you have something worth merit to offer Cecily, I'm all for the one-on-ones. If not, do not even think about it."

The Goddess's words hung in the air with warning dripping off each syllable. Crossing her would be the very last thing someone would do. Shiva blanched and bowed to her Goddess.

Lilith pulled a jeweled dagger from her belt, sliced her palm open then held it out to me. "Shall we?"

We'd done this before. If she believed it would help, I would do it again. She'd explained that her blood gave me a power boost—best when used for others. I'd be hard pressed to think this was normal behavior, but it was growing clear that it was par for the course in the Demon world.

I took the dagger. It felt heavy and vibrated in my hand. The enchantment was obvious. We were back in Crazy Town. Immortals were insane. Sucking in a quick breath, I went for it. The razor-sharp dagger sliced my palm like a hot knife through frozen butter. My blood spurted. I stared as it dripped down my fingertips and onto the blades of grass at my feet. The sensation was searingly painful, but I sucked it up and refused to wince.

Lilith clasped her hand in mine. Her gaze was focused, intense and somewhat frightening. She stood as still as a statue—a beautiful, terrifying Goddess made of stone. I thought I might pass out from blood loss. Of course, because life was batshit nuts, we ignited—just like we had the first time my mother had given me her blood. Our joined hands caught fire. It was as black as the Darkness. I watched in fascination as the flames moved up our arms in a circular motion. It was a mini tornado of fire. The most shocking part was that it didn't hurt—at all. The rush was quick and all-consuming followed by a sense of absolute calm.

It ended so quickly I felt a bizarre sense of sorrow. Lilith removed her hand from mine and smiled. I looked down at my palm as the skin knitted back together immediately. I sure as hell hoped I didn't need surgery in the future. My healing abilities would freak a human doctor out. Hell, I was freaked out.

"Shall we?" Dagon inquired.

"Sure," I replied. I had nothing to lose and hopefully a lot to gain. "Who's up first?"

Dagon smiled and gestured to follow him. "I'll go first, Goddess Cecily."

I smiled back and accompanied the Demon around the side of the cottage. It was tempting to ask Dagon to go last since he was the kindest, but the Immortals seemed to have a method to their madness. I was just along for the ride.

THE TRAINING FACILITY WAS LARGER THAN THE COTTAGE BY A lot. From the outside it looked like a random metal warehouse. Inside was a different story. The walls and floors were padded. It reminded me of a film I'd done where I'd been wrongly accused of murder, thrown into a padded cell and left to rot by the real murderer. Of course, due to the magic of the movies and a really bad script, I escaped the padded room through a vent in the ceiling and crawled about a mile to safety. From there I plotted my revenge and took the bad guy down in a blaze of glory.

I was pretty sure the ending of this scene I was about to take part in wouldn't be as easy as the crappy movie. Real life had a way of humbling people.

Folding chairs lined the walls. A running track circled the perimeter. Weights and exercise machines were spread out at the far end of the massive open room. That was normal. The cache of deadly weapons in a glass case that went from the floor to the vaulted ceiling was anything but. It was unclear what some of the weapons were. Fifi would know. I wished like crazy my grenade-loving Succubus bodyguard was with me.

I swallowed back my fear and followed Dagon in. He sat down at a table and indicated I should take the seat across from him. I glanced back to see if Lilith, Shiva or Abaddon had joined us. They had not.

Feeling a little unsteady on my feet, I walked to the table and sat down.

"Are we going to fight?" I asked, steeling myself to be ready.

Dagon was a badass of epic proportions. There was a reason he was Lilith's second in command. The fact that he was nice made him more of a badass.

"I certainly hope not," he replied with a chuckle.

I sighed audibly with relief. He chuckled again.

"There's something even more powerful than brute force," he explained. "Those who jump to violence first oftentimes lose. Decapitation is permanent. However, stealth and stillness are often wiser."

It felt a little like I was in school. Granted, the subject matter was different... Dagon waited for me to speak.

I didn't disappoint. "Knowledge is more powerful than violence."

His smile grew wider and I preened under his approval. "Correct. And you are missing much of it. Ask me questions, child."

I nodded and racked my brain for questions that wouldn't sound stupid. Wait. No question was stupid. My ego didn't come into this at all. My dad's life was on the line as well as mine. Although, I did have a question bugging me that didn't really pertain...

"This place—the cottage," I said, knowing that my curiosity would get the best of me if I didn't satisfy it. Having scattered focus would be counterproductive... or that was what I told myself. "Do you come here often?"

"No," he replied evenly. "The cottage belongs to Lilith. I've never entered it until today. The training facility has a guest house behind it. When others are here, that's where we stay."

"Mmkay," I said, wanting to know more—like if Abaddon was welcome inside. "And do *others* go into the cottage? You know, besides Lilith?"

"Beating around the bush will get you nowhere, Cecily," Dagon commented dryly. "But to answer the query that you

seek a reply for, the response is no. The cottage is a sacred
place for the Goddess, and only the Goddess. Until recently,
none of us were aware of your existence. I was shocked and
honored to be invited today."

I didn't know why his answer calmed me, but it did. It
was strange enough to think that Lilith had created the
shrine. It would be creepy to imagine Abaddon seeing
images of me since I was a child. "How long ago did Lilith
get this place?"

"Forty years. Right after you were born," Dagon said. "I'd
suggest moving on to subjects that might be more
conducive to helping you in your quest."

He was correct. My need to know the backstory came
from being an actress my entire life. Details fascinated me.
If I lived past tomorrow, I'd ask for more. Living past
tomorrow was not a guarantee. The Demon was offering
knowledge to help me. I switched tracks and dove in. My
bruised inner child would have to wait.

"Are you aware of the others in the game?" I asked.
"Stella Stevens, Corny Crackers, Jonny Jones, Moon Sunny
Swartz and umm..." Shit I didn't know PT Bitch's real
name.

"Irma Stoutwagon," Dagon supplied. "And yes, I am
aware of all of them."

My mouth formed a perfect O. "Shut the front door," I
said with a laugh. "That is *not* her name."

"I assure you it is," he replied with a shudder. "A very
unpleasant Demon. I believe she has a stage name, but Irma
Stoutwagon is her given name."

"Holy cow," I muttered with a giggle. Hell, I didn't have

to call her PT Bitch anymore. Irma Stoutwagon was far worse. I tucked that piece of info away for future use. "Who are they loyal to? Lilith or Pandora?"

"Excellent question," Dagon said, making me feel great. "Neither. There are select Demons who are loyal only unto themselves."

"Is that legal?"

He shrugged. "If your elected president isn't the person you voted for, do you feel a loyalty to him or her?"

"Well, sadly, we haven't had a her yet, but I see your point," I acknowledged. "The Demon world is a democratic society?"

"No," Dagon said. "If one were to compare it to something understandable to the human model, it would be more of a royal society. There are two factions of the Demon culture—dark and light. Pandora is the dark and Lilith is the light. Without both, no balance can be maintained. No matter who a Demon is loyal to, they must adhere to the laws of our kind."

I nodded. Abaddon had said as much. Although, it did seem like a rather lawless society. "Is it good or bad that the others in the game have no loyalty to a Goddess?"

Dagon considered the question for a moment. "It's neither here nor there. Keep in mind they are all powerful, but flawed," he finally replied. "I've read the contract. It's appalling."

"Agreed, but I'm doing it."

"As would I," he replied. "Choose your ally carefully and never turn your back on them."

"Trusting any of them will be difficult."

Dagon reached across the table for my hand. I placed my hand in his. He gently squeezed. "Self-trust is the first secret of success."

I squeezed back. "Ralph Waldo Emerson."

"Ahh," he said with a chuckle. "Deadly and smart—an excellent combination. Never forget... it's better to trust the man who is frequently in error than the one who is never in doubt."

"Eric Sevareid," I said instantly. I mulled over the quote and tried to figure out which of the five would be the best ally to choose. None of them were great. "What else have you got for me, Dagon?"

The Demon let go of my hand and leaned back in his chair. "Be an optimist, Cecily. Be the Demon who understands that taking a step backward after taking a step forward is not a fault. It's a cha-cha."

A giggle escaped my mouth. The discussion was all over the place. Having a Demon tell me to be an optimist was surreal. "So, I can just dance my way to the ending I choose?"

Dagon raised a brow, but there was amusement in his gaze. "In a simplistic way, yes. However, the dance is deadly and the consequences are dire."

I didn't feel like giggling anymore. "How is Pandora able to get away with this? She's supposed to be in Demon time-out."

"That shall be dealt with," he replied. "She has gone against the Keeper of Fate's decree—a very unwise move."

"Why can't it be dealt with now?" I demanded. It would solve a host of problems, the main one being my dad.

"Lilith has decreed no one shall touch her until Bill is safe."

I sat with that. I agreed completely, but at the same time I was devastated. My mother was willing to risk my life for my dad's. Confusion at my feelings of anger washed over me. I was willing to do the same thing, but that was my choice. The realization that I was expendable to her was devastating.

Gripping the edge of the table until my knuckles turned white, I swallowed all the harsh and ugly words that were on the tip of my tongue. Dagon didn't need to hear about my abandonment issues. To him they would be ridiculous. He was older than dirt and most likely agreed with what Lilith had done. I was a liability to all of them.

Maybe my mother wanted me to die to save the man who completed her. If I was gone, Man-mom would no longer be in danger.

I didn't realize my hands were sparking until the table went up in flames. Dagon snapped his fingers and put out the fire.

"Let me ask you a question," Dagon queried calmly, behaving as if the smoldering wood was standard. "Is there *anything* that would stop you from going after your father?"

Speaking without yelling was hard. Inhaling deeply, I shook my head. "No. Nothing."

"Do you think Lilith and Abaddon know this?"

"Yes," I hissed.

"Then your ire is misplaced."

I let that sink in. I'd refused to back down when Abaddon was in danger even though Lilith tried to forbid it.

I'd only known Abaddon for a very short period of time, but he'd saved me and I owed him. I was also in love with him and unfortunately still was. I'd known and loved my dad my entire life. It was a no brainer that I would rescue Man-mom. My love for my dad was unconditional and strong. He and my brother were my whole world.

Lilith knew there was no stopping me. So, instead, it appeared she was doing her best to help. I tried to make the realization erase the thought that she would sacrifice me. The logical side of my brain accepted it. The illogical side was crushed. I was forty, but the hurt child buried deep inside me was still there.

Nodding jerkily, I let go of the smoking table and put my hands in my lap. "Got it," I said in a tight voice.

Dagon eyed me for a long moment. "I don't think you fully do, but only time will convince you of that. Time marches at its own pace, child."

"This isn't a therapy session," I snapped then let my chin fall to my chest. Being rude to Dagon was wildly unneces-sary. The man was trying to help me. It was tough shit if I didn't like what he had to say. "Sorry. That was uncalled for."

"Nothing relevant should be apologized for, Cecily. Get it out now so the focus will be where it is needed."

Dagon was like a Buddha of sorts. His calm and well-reasoned manner was almost hypnotic. His intuition was spot on and he was kind.

"Thank you," I told him. "But I stand by my apology. You're not the source of my anger."

"You will not be punished *for* your anger; you will be punished *by* your anger."

I grinned and shook my head. I was correct in my comparison of the Demon to Buddha. He'd just quoted the man. "You like Buddha?"

"Very much," Dagon replied with a smile. "And in the sage words of the Dalai Lama—Generally speaking, if a human being never shows anger, then I think something is wrong."

"I do agree with that."

Dagon stood up and crossed his arms over his chest. "We are not able to help you in person per the contract," he said. "But there will be signs."

I squinted at him. "Can you be more specific?"

"Signs," he repeated. "Look for the signs. It's how your mother will guide you."

I groaned, but tried to find a loophole that would make his cryptic message make more sense. "Will she talk to me in my mind?"

He shook his head. "Signs."

Well, crap. "So, I'll feel her and know what to do?"

"Signs," he said again.

I closed my eyes and willed myself not to be a butthole. Dagon was making it difficult. "Okay," I ground out through clenched teeth. "I'll look for freaking signs."

"Excellent," he replied. "The more anger you carry, the less likely you are able to love."

I was stumped. I had no clue who the quote was from. "Who said that?"

"I did," Dagon said.

His sage words hit me hard. Candy Vargo had banged into my head that love conquers evil. Dagon had clearly stated that anger dulls love. I didn't love Pandora. I never would. If that was the magic bullet, I was screwed.

Pressing my lips together, I nodded to Dagon. "Thank you, I'll keep that in mind."

"I believe in you, Goddess Cecily," he said with a deep bow. "Now you must believe in yourself."

In a poof of silver mist, Dagon disappeared. Inhaling deeply, I waited for my next one-on-one.

It went from weird to weirder as Shiva poofed in and dumped a bag of makeup onto the table.

"Get ready to be wowed, bitch," she snapped.

I rolled my eyes. Apparently, I was about to get a makeover.

CHAPTER SIX

THERE WERE ENOUGH COSMETICS ON THE TABLE TO LAST A
year—lipstick, blush, foundation, perfume, eyeshadow,
pencils in every shade and all the tools to apply the potions.
If Shiva thought getting dolled up would help me defeat
Pandora, she was a bigger jackass than I already thought
she was.

I sighed loudly and waited. The sun hadn't risen yet, so
there was still time to get prepared—and by that I didn't
mean getting my face painted up like a hooker. I was
surprised I wasn't exhausted since I hadn't slept. Although, I
was hungry. I'd solve that issue after Shiva made me look
like a clown.

"I hate you," she began in a neutral tone.

"Ditto," I replied with a bland smile.

She hissed and kicked the chair. With my mouth open, I
watched her have a fit. The Demon paced back and forth for

a few minutes and let every swear word she knew rip. It was mighty impressive. However, I was over it.

"This is a waste of my time," I ground out as my hands tingled and began to spark dangerously. It took some will power not to let my purple fire swords pop out. "I don't know why Lilith trusts you. I don't. One would assume someone as *old* as you are would have learned to control their anger. Clearly, that isn't the case. Leave. Now. You can walk out on your own accord or I can help you. The choice is yours. And trust me, you don't want me to help you."

"You can't tell me to leave, bitch," she snarled. "I'm Shiva."

I tilted my head in mock confusion. "Pretty sure I just did, *Shiva.*"

Her eyes narrowed and she bared her teeth. "I'll fight you for him."

I groaned and laughed. "You are unreal. If you want Abaddon, go and get him. I have no claim to him."

"Yes, you do," she screeched. "He should be mine."

I squinted at her. "Do Lilith and Abaddon know the bullshit you're spouting in here?"

Her eyes grew wide with fear for a moment. She covered it quickly. "We shall fight. If I have to kill you in self-defense, she will not banish me. I've been loyal to my Goddess always."

This wasn't going like I thought it would. At all. The crazed imbecile wanted to end me... over a man. It was a game I would not play. Not today. Not ever.

"You think you'll get away with killing me?" I inquired so calmly she looked alarmed.

"I don't think," she announced. "I know."

"Good luck with that," I replied.

"Bitch," she shrieked and produced her fire sword.

I stood and raised my arms over my head. A frigid wind blasted through the room knocking the Demon on her ass.

I smiled.

She didn't.

"To whom it may concern, this is a wish for the Demon Shiva," I began as she scrambled to her feet and backed away in fury and uncertainty. I waved my hand and trapped her in a bubble. I wasn't fucking around and I was insanely relieved that the bubble worked. I was pulling the magic out of my ass. Fighting her wasn't on the agenda. I was saving that for Pandora. With a snap of my fingers her sword disappeared. Her scream of outrage was jarring. "I have a mission. I don't need a beautician. There's a bad Demon scheming who wants me dead. Pandora's a whore-a, her evil must not spread." I'd used a similar line in another spell, but it seemed to apply here too. I wasn't sure if it was a no-no to reuse spells, but again, I was winging it. My rhyming wasn't stellar, but as a newbie spellcaster, I didn't have time to be concerned. "I need the bitchy Demon Shiva as an ally. If she chooses to defy, I will bid her a permanent goodbye. Shiva shall obey or a high price she will pay."

The Demon was on her knees in the bubble. Her demeanor had changed drastically. She appeared meek. I didn't buy it for a second. Hate was a strong emotion and she had it for me in spades. Jealously on top of it was a shitty and deadly combo when dealing with Demons. I glared at her. She couldn't meet my gaze. If Lilith had allowed her in here, she must have something to offer. While I wanted to send her away, I didn't. Man-mom's life was more important than banishing and humiliating Shiva. Of course, that didn't mean I wouldn't kick her ass in the future, but not today.

"Fate will not be destroyed by hate. Shiva's power shall be bound by the Goddess Cecily's mandate." I paused and gathered my thoughts. Being specific was key. "My destiny is mine to shape. I will not permit a useless and pathetic Immortal to let my focus escape." I walked over to the bubble and pointed at the cowering idiot. "You will teach me what you know. Your rabid hatred, you will let go. Far too much is at stake. The spell will last until I command it to break. Thank you and have a good day."

With another wave of my hand, I disintegrated the bubble. I didn't expect the thunder and lightning, but it was a nice touch.

Shiva was still on the ground. I wasn't sure why, but I felt a little sorry for her. She didn't deserve my pity, but it was mine to give if I so chose.

"Get up," I said flatly. "If the makeup is useful, explain it. If you truly just came in here to mess with me, you're free to leave. And you can explain your behavior to Lilith."

She got to her feet and bowed to me. I really wasn't into the unsettling respect stuff, but it was better than her challenging me.

Shiva walked over to the table, righted the chair she'd kicked over and seated herself. I joined her. She was subdued. I watched her covertly test her power. Nothing happened. The nasty piece of work was at my mercy. Right now, being a Goddess didn't suck.

"Start talking," I instructed in an icy tone.

"All of the makeup can kill or immobilize," she said, staring at the table. "The lipstick is a laser that will incapacitate a Demon for twenty-four hours."

"How does it work?" I asked, quickly dropping a see-through barrier between us just in case she decided to test it out on me. Her power might be muted, but she could still use a weapon. I had places to go and a dad to save. If she messed with that, I would end her. I didn't care how much Lilith liked and trusted her.

"Open the cap, aim it at the enemy and squeeze the tube," she replied, looking crushed that I'd created a wall of safety. "Is that necessary?"

I rolled my eyes. "Do you expect me to trust you?" I demanded.

"Umm... no. I guess not," she replied, sounding defensive.

Too bad, so sad. Trust with Demons came with proof. She'd only proven that she wanted me dead so far. "What else do you have there?"

"A lot," she replied.

She wasn't kidding. The brushes were daggers. The foundation was liquid poison that could be dispensed with the sponges that turned into tiny revolvers. The eyelash curlers were grenades that detonated when thrown. The perfume rendered one invisible for ten minutes. The pencils were shivs. The eye shadow, when ground, could blind. The bag that stored the makeup could be melted down and used to heal.

I stared in surprise at the colorful arsenal. "Where did you get this stuff?"

"It's mine," she answered.

"Not what I asked," I shot back. "Who makes it and do other Demons have it?"

Shiva shook her head and smiled proudly. It was kind of creepy. "No other Demons have it. I created it. All of it."

Squinting at her, I wasn't sure if I bought her story. "I have a bridge for sale."

Her smile disappeared. "Fuck you."

"I'd rather not."

The Demon wanted to come at me so badly. She balled her fists, and her eyes glowed red. "I have ten PhDs," she snarled. "Physics, Biochemistry, Nuclear Physics and Pharmacology to name a few. Biological weapons are my hobby."

I was at a loss for words. Batshit crazy and book smart was a hell of a terrifying combo. I now understood why she was valuable to Lilith. I didn't like her. I didn't trust her, but if she was offering me her cosmetic weaponry, she'd gained back a few points.

"Have you tested the makeup?"

"Most of it," she admitted after a long pause.

I raised a brow and waited.

"The lipstick works. It's reusable up to three times," she finally said. "The eyelash curler is definitely a grenade— single use only. The pencils are shivs, but don't do much damage. The other items, I'm not sure. I was hoping you could test them for me."

I rolled my eyes. A failed test could mean death… for me. She knew that and I knew that.

"Now I know why no one likes you," I muttered.

"People like me," she said, wildly offended.

"Actually, they don't."

"Says who?" she demanded.

"Ophelia," I replied.

She slammed her fists onto the table scattering the makeup. The perfume bottle exploded and the liquid covered her legs. Her appendages disappeared. Well, that was one more item that worked. We both stared in shock at where her legs used to be.

Shiva immediately stood up to make sure that the invisible appendages still worked. They did. Although, she looked absurd. "Fuck," she grumbled then glared at me. "I have lots of friends."

"Name them," I said.

She was bewildered… and pissed… and hurt. "Fine, bitch. I have no friends and I don't care. Friends are bullshit and a waste of time."

"You're wrong, but I'm pretty sure you already know that," I said, waving my hand and dropping the barrier. "And let me state for the record, if you use any of your weapons on me and keep me from saving my dad, I will destroy you. It'll be slow, painful and very bloody. If you luck out and actually kill me, I'll haunt you until the end of time. Your life will be beyond miserable and I'll send your sorry ass over the cliff into insanity. You'll rue the day you were born."

Shiva had the audacity to look impressed. I'd actually stolen a few of the lines from a horror movie I'd done back in the day. The Demon didn't understand kindness, but she did seem to dig the threat of violence.

"You can have Abaddon," she said in a snippy tone. "I don't want him."

I wanted to point out that he didn't want her either, but figured that would be counterproductive. Instead, I stayed silent. Abaddon wasn't an object to be passed around. He was a man—a man who I'd destroyed my chances with. However, Shiva obviously hadn't gotten the memo on that. Far be it from me to enlighten her. It was heinous enough that I had to live with the fact that I'd blown up my chance at happiness. Having the violent Demon gloat over it wasn't in the plan.

Shiva rocked back and forth awkwardly for a moment. It was bizarre since her legs weren't visible. "Would you like to go to lunch after you save your father and kick Pandora's ass?" she inquired casually as she packed the makeup bag with several lipsticks and the five eyelash curler grenades she'd brought.

"I'm sorry, what?" I asked, certain I'd misheard.

"Forget it," she snapped. "I was trying to be nice."

"You started out this little session by telling me you hated me and that you wanted to end me in the name of self-defense. Call me crazy, but a lunch date isn't the logical end of the scene."

The Demon ran her hands through her hair. She was beautiful, but that only ran skin deep. "Everyone is afraid of me," she snapped. "No one ever asks me to do anything." Her voice rose a few octaves as she kept going. "Do you have any idea what it's like to be well over ten thousand years old and never get asked to do anything? NO! No, you don't. You're a freaking movie star and the daughter of a Goddess. You probably get invited to everything. I just figured since you could actually kill me, you might want to be my friend... or at least a semi-hostile acquaintance. I'm letting you use my makeup. I would think that would merit a lunch, bitch."

Her logic was beyond skewed. I almost laughed. "Why are you letting me use your makeup?"

Shiva's face screwed up and she turned an unflattering red. "Because."

"Because?"

She stomped her foot and spewed enough filthy words to make a sailor proud. "Because Lilith made me," she bellowed. "However, I did it. Five points for me."

I knew I'd live to regret what I was about to say... if I lived past tomorrow. Candy Vargo had said love conquers evil. Shiva was on the evil side. I'd be hard pressed to say I loved her, but I could try to like her. Maybe... "Fine. We'll go to lunch. Once. If you're not a gaping hole of ass, we might go to the movies."

"Some place public where others will see us," she bargained. "And maybe end up in the tabloids."

"Seriously?" I asked.

"Yes," she barked, then tamped it back. "And I'd like Slash Gordon's number."

We'd just taken a hard left into Weirdsville. "He's an asshole."

Shiva shrugged. "So am I."

"Word," I muttered. "It's a deal."

She handed me the bag and smiled. "I still hate you, but I think we'll be good friends."

Before I could utter an appalled response, the Demon poofed away.

This night couldn't get any more bizarre.

Oh yes it could.

CHAPTER SEVEN

ABADDON DIDN'T POOF IN.

He walked through the door.

My heart sped up and my mouth went dry. If I could have punched myself in the head without looking like I'd lost it, I would have. Knowing that I'd destroyed us before we'd really begun was heart wrenching. It gave me the feeling of burning dread in my chest—the same sensation I got when I reminded myself I wasn't human anymore. Neither my heritage nor what I'd done could be altered.

Apologizing seemed asinine. Trying to reverse the spell would be psychotic. Knowledge was power and I'd neglected to search it out before I'd jumped the gun. To cut myself a little slack, the compulsion thing was off-putting and bizarre, but we weren't here to hash out how unknowingly shortsighted I'd been. Abaddon no longer loved me. We were here to prepare me to save my dad. Period.

The Demon was physically gorgeous. His black hair was

slightly too long and sexy in a messy way. He wore Armani as well as he wore jeans and t-shirts. Abaddon, or Dick, as I occasionally liked to call him due to his obnoxious personality, was both frustratingly rude and good to the core. His insides were more beautiful than his outer exterior. Sadly, I'd never get the chance to know him better and I had no one to blame but me. As hard as I tried to tell myself that I didn't understand the Demon mythology about finding your other half, it still broke my heart. Life was so much less complicated when I was just a former child star who was trying to make a comeback at forty in a world full of Botox and bullshit.

Sucking back my regret was difficult but doable. I simply pictured Man-mom's face. My dad was my reality. Man-mom loved me unconditionally. There was nothing I could do to destroy my father's love for me. Or, for that matter, mine for him. Getting him out of Pandora's clutches, even if I had to die to accomplish it, was my only goal. My feelings for Abaddon would fade with time. I hoped. If not, I had a long life of remorse ahead. Of course, it might be moot since I could be six feet under shortly. Whatever. What didn't kill you made you stronger according to Kelly Clarkson.

In his hands, Abaddon carried a large tray. His eyes were glued to mine as he strode across the training room to the table. I was uncomfortable under his gaze and felt naked. I looked down to make sure I wasn't.

Thankfully, my clothes were still on my body. Sadly, my heart was probably perched on my sleeve.

"Food," he said emotionlessly as he put the tray on the table. "You need to eat."

I sighed then groaned with relief. I was starving.

It was fleeting, but I thought Abaddon cracked a tiny smile. It was probably my imagination, but I was an actress. I lived in an imaginary world most of the time. It was turning out that my wild and warped imagination was safer than my real life. Who would have thunk...

"Thank you." My voice sounded formal and wooden. Hanging on to my self-dignity was hard when it was just him and me. Being reserved was my armor. Letting emotions get in the way would be embarrassing for both of us.

Abaddon removed the ornate silver covers from the plates. The food was served on exquisite porcelain China, and the drinks were in sparkling crystal glasses. The irony that it was hamburgers and french fries made me smile. My stomach rumbled. I grabbed a starched white linen napkin and dug in.

"Oh my God," I mumbled with a mouthful of burger. "This is insane."

"Slow down," he instructed curtly. "Choking to death wouldn't be your best move."

I swallowed a big bite and took a swig of water to wash it down. "Is that possible?"

"Is what possible?"

"I'm a Demon. Can I really choke to death?" I questioned.

He scrubbed his hand over his face. I wasn't sure if he

was trying not to laugh, hiding a smile or just disgusted by me. "No. A Demon can choke, but not to death."

"Good to know," I said, taking another huge bite.

He ignored my crappy manners and removed a cover from a bowl of fresh berries and a plate of warm brownies. The smell was heavenly. I reached greedily for a brownie then jerked my hand back.

"Are they safe?" I asked warily.

The Demon was confused. I didn't blame him. In my experience, brownies were somewhat dangerous. My brother, the fabulous functioning pothead, only ever made Mary Jane brownies. I'd trained myself to avoid them for decades. After ingesting one of Sean's brownies and accidentally getting as high as a kite before a meeting with a major studio about a TV holding deal, I'd steered clear of the chocolate treat. I'd laughed like a hyena throughout the entire hour. The memory of screaming that I was going to pee my pants while one of the execs outlined the contract points was a mind-numbing nightmare. Needless to say, the deal was axed.

"Define safe," Abaddon said, still perplexed as he picked up a brownie and examined it.

"Umm…" I felt like an idiot, but I'd started it. I had to finish it. "They're not pot brownies? Right?"

His eyebrows shot up in surprise and he laughed. The sound made me light-headed and breathless. He was handsome all the time, but when he laughed, he was otherworldly gorgeous. "They are *not* pot brownies," he finally said after he pulled himself back together.

I nodded, embarrassed. However, Candy Vargo had said

no question was dumb. That was debatable at the moment, but getting high wasn't on the table. Even though the brownies looked delicious, I was too mortified to eat one now. Abaddon had no problem and ate three.

"Are you here to teach me anything?" I asked, picking at the french fries and drawing circles in the ketchup.

He turned the question back on me. "What do you want to learn, Cecily?"

I rolled my eyes. He was a game player. I wasn't. "Well, Dick... how to defeat Pandora would be nice to know. How to avoid getting offed by assassins. How to give back my Demon card and go back to my old life. Any of that would do."

"The third query is absurd and pathetic," he said tightly. "It's quite clear that you despise what you are, but that isn't something I care to help you with."

I blew out a long breath and regretted my wording. My fate as a Demon had been set. Controlling my destiny was my job. Calling him Dick was juvenile, but he rattled my brain and good sense. I couldn't take my words back so I danced the cha-cha like Dagon had suggested. One step back meant it was now time to take one step forward. "What about Pandora?"

"She's dangerous and wants you dead," he ground out. "I don't like this at all. I don't want you to do it."

I shook my head. "That's not on the table for discussion."

"There are other ways, Cecily," he insisted, pinning me with a gaze that was as hot as it was scary.

I picked up a brownie and took a bite. It was delicious. "These other ways," I said, swallowing and putting the treat down. "Are they surefire as far as keeping my dad from harm?"

He stayed silent. That was all the answer I needed.

"Look," I told him, pushing the tray away. I was no longer hungry. I fully understood that no one in Lilith's camp wanted me to play Pandora's game. I was doing it anyway. In my heart, I knew my dad would step in front of a speeding train for both me and Sean. I was willing to do the same for him. "I don't know if you understand unconditional love, but I do."

Abaddon growled and glared at me. Again, I found that hot. I needed my head examined.

Talking about love might not be the best example considering our brief but intense history, but walking on eggshells was ridiculous. I had less than twelve hours before I had to report to my deadly job. I wasn't going to get talked out of it no matter what anyone said or how loudly they growled.

"I love my dad," I started again. "He shouldn't be involved in any of this. He's human and innocent. If Pandora wanted to get to me, she succeeded. I'm also aware that I shouldn't end her even though I want to with everything I am."

Abaddon pressed his temples. "You couldn't end her if you tried."

"Don't underestimate dread necessity," I shot right back. "I'm willing to go down with her."

The Demon stood up and walked away from me. He raised his hands over his head and blew the entire back wall out of the training center. Steel girders and metal tumbled to the ground with a loud screeching crash. He wasn't done. As the metal lay in a twisted pile, he snapped his fingers and melted it to goo.

It was an impressive show of destruction.

Abaddon walked back to the table as calm as a cucumber. There was something to be said for getting it all out so it didn't consume you.

"You done?" I asked.

"Depends," he replied in a clipped tone. "I can't help you if you do this. I can't be there to protect you. I can't guide you." He slammed his hands down on the table. It cracked in half and the food, China and crystal went flying. "I am not okay with this," he bellowed. His eyes glowed red and his body was wound as tight as I'd ever seen it.

If I didn't know better, it sounded like he cared. I did know better. I was the Goddess Lilith's daughter. His loyalty was to her. I was part of her whether I wanted to acknowledge it or not. But more importantly to me, I was part of Man-mom and he was an innocent pawn in a shitty and life-threatening game.

"I'm going," I said flatly. "If you have words of wisdom or any advice, I'll take it. If you're just going to obliterate the training area, we're done."

He leaned back in his chair and crossed his arms over his chest. His expression was smug. I wanted to slap it off of his face. "And that's where you're wrong, Cecily."

His words were loaded. Clearly, we needed to get some stuff out of the way. "I'm sorry."

"For?" he inquired coldly.

My anger bubbled up from somewhere deep inside. Yes,

I was heartbroken over the spell I'd cast that made him lose his compulsion for me. I'd done it for him. It seemed stupidly unfair that he was forced by some kind of archaic magic to want and love me.

"Pardon me." I got up and walked over to the left side of the training area. No one had freaked out that Abaddon had blown up part of the building. Honestly, it seemed like pretty normal behavior for these whack jobs. And since I'd joined the whack job club—albeit unwillingly—I was going to take advantage of the perks.

Wiggling my fingers then slashing my arms through the air, I detonated all the workout equipment. The loud boom as the treadmill and elliptical blasted through the wall made me jump. It sounded like a ten-car pileup. However, I had to admit, I felt less stressed. Property destruction was cathartic.

I marched back over to the table, but refused to sit down. My mind felt chaotic and I wanted to cry. Badasses didn't cry. Candy Vargo would not be proud of me right now.

"Are you done?" Abaddon inquired, repeating my question from earlier.

"I'm just getting started," I informed him. "If it wasn't obvious to you, I didn't know about the prehistoric way Demons find each other. So, what I did, I did for you… and me, jackass. I'm kind of big into the free will thing. If you're going to continue to be a dick about it, you should leave. I said I was sorry. That's all I've got. My focus is my dad. Not you. Not me."

He inhaled slowly and then stood. He began to pace back

and forth. I had no freaking clue what the man was thinking. Several times he opened his mouth to speak then thought better of it and continued pacing.

"Are you okay?" I asked. Abaddon was rarely at a loss for words since I'd met him. This was way out of character.

"No. I'm not," he replied. His eyes were red and practically spitting sparks.

I looked down at the floor. I couldn't undo what I'd done. Abaddon was angry and hurt. It was my fault. Maybe with time we could be friends. It would be hard, but I was willing to try. Being an asshole wasn't my usual MO. Humiliating myself wasn't either, but for Man-mom I would beg on my knees. "Please help me. Have you ever been so scared of losing someone you love that you would go to the ends of the world to save them? That's how I feel. It consumes me beyond reason. You know my dad. You like my dad. He considers you a friend. Lilith loves my dad. I know none of you can aid me when I'm playing the game. And yes, I am scared to go it alone, but I'm terrified of what will happen if I don't. That's how much I love my dad. I know you despise me, but I'll owe you. Please help me, Abaddon."

"I'd like to take you over my knee and spank you," he ground out.

My mouth worked before my brain caught wind of what was coming out. "That's kind of hot," I said then slapped my hands over my mouth in horror. I spoke through splayed fingers as I felt my face heat up. "I take that back. Never said it."

ROBYN PETERMAN

Abaddon went from pissed to intrigued… very intrigued.

Shit.

He sat back down at the broken table and pointed to the seat across from him. "Sit."

"I'm not a dog."

"Never said you were."

I rolled my eyes and sat down.

"You like word games," he said, stating the obvious.

I twisted my dark hair in my fingers and sighed. These Immortals were so cryptic. It sucked all kinds of butt. "Yes. I like word games."

"You say a word. I'll comment," Abaddon said. "Think of it as an exchange of knowledge. You'll go first then I'll take my turn."

"Fine." If it was all I could get, I'd accept it. I was going to be specific and I'd start with the others in the game. "Stella Stevens."

"Backstabber who can sense when danger is imminent."

"Awesome," I muttered. "Corny Crackers."

"Perverted, violent and can fly."

"Seriously?" I asked surprised—not surprised about the pervert part, but the flying was a shock. "Is that a normal Demon thingie?"

"Thingie?" he asked with a quirked brow.

"Yes," I snapped. "Thingie."

He was amused. I wasn't.

"No, it's not a normal thingie."

"Can I fly?" I asked. I would be totally down with that. My dreams throughout my life had been filled with flying.

"I have no clue. Can you?"

I blew out a loud raspberry. I'd check with Ophelia on the flying thingie. She was a lot nicer and more forthcoming than Abaddon.

"Jonny Jones," I said, sticking to the basics.

"Not as stupid as he wants you to believe," he warned. "Can render himself invisible."

"Shut the front door," I said with a groan.

"However," Abaddon continued. "It's detectable. When the Demon goes invisible there's the faint scent of rotten eggs."

"For real?" I wrinkled my nose. I was familiar with the scent of rotten eggs. Sean and Man-mom were seriously lax about cleaning out their fridge. Now that Uncle Joe was back in all his naked ghostly glory, the food in my house and theirs was up to date.

"For real," he confirmed with an expression of distaste. "If you smell it, beware. Jonny Jones is nearby in a concealed form."

I nodded and gagged a little. "If I'm standing behind him, am I invisible as well?"

Abaddon raised an impressed brow. "Yes."

I couldn't help the grin that pulled at my lips, but I refused to let my mouth form a full smile. Gloating was for losers. Candy Vargo said I was a badass. Plus, there was more knowledge to be gained. "Moon Sunny Swartz."

"Zero fear of repercussion."

That wasn't a shock. The woman pulled idiotic pranks that had almost landed her in the slammer multiple times. She was persona non grata in Hollywood.

"The Demon can also attract danger by humming."

"That's a good thing?" I asked with an annoyed tilt of my head.

"Depends," he replied. "If you tire of waiting for your enemy, you might be in a stronger position if they come to you."

I took that one in and mulled it over. The point was excellent. If I chose Moon as my ally—even though the thought gave me gas—I could draw the assassins to me instead of hunting them down or letting them discover me first. The upper hand could mean the difference between breathing and not breathing.

Although, Corny could potentially fly me out of a sure death situation, Jonny could conceal me and Stella could sense danger headed our way. Crap. I wasn't sure who was the most valuable. I was damn good with my purple fire swords, but if I didn't see the enemy coming, I was toast.

"PT Bitch." I'd left the worst for last. "I mean, Irma Stoutwagon."

"Bad news." Abaddon confirmed what I'd already known. "Although, she's vicious in battle and can shape shift."

I squinted at him in disbelief. "Into what?"

He shuddered. "A mouse."

I laughed. He didn't.

Abaddon was flabbergasted. "You think that's funny?"

"Very."

"You're not terrified of mice?" he demanded, shocked to the core.

"Umm... no," I replied. "I don't love them, but they don't

scare me. They're kind of cute. Well, the tiny ones are. I had a pet hamster named Keith when I was a kid—not a mouse, but he was sweet, little and furry."

The Demon's mouth dropped open. What the heck was going on here? I'd seen the man lop off the heads of Pandora's flaming assholes without pause. He'd also chanted in a weird dead language and popped a bunch of bad Immortals like they were ticks. I was mighty confused. "Are you afraid of mice?"

Again, he shuddered. The big strong man paled. "No, but it's taken me over ten thousand years to be able to tolerate them."

It was my turn to be open mouthed. Was I being punked? "Demons are terrified of mice?"

The concept was so absurd, I laughed.

Abaddon wasn't as amused. "The short answer is yes. Unless a Demon has done desensitization training, they can't tolerate the sight. There are only three others, aside from you, apparently, that I know of besides myself who have beaten the fear."

"Who?"

"The Goddess Lilith, the Grim Reaper and Dagon. And I'd have to make an educated guess that Irma Stoutwagon has no issue with mice."

This had to be bullshit. It was beyond nuts that killing machines were scared of a little mouse. "Mmkay," I said, not buying the rickety bridge he was selling. "What happens when Demons are around a mouse?"

"Chaos," Abaddon informed me. "They'll kill each other to get away."

Still unsure if he was pulling my leg, I played along. "And are other Demons aware that Irma Stoutwagon can shift into a mouse?"

He shook his head. "Highly doubtful. If they were, she would have been decapitated eons ago."

"It's crazy that she can shift into a rodent."

Abaddon looked like he was going to hurl. "Can you abstain from using the word rodent?"

Biting back a grin was really hard. "Sure. So, Demons are like a herd of elephants around mice?"

"That's a myth," Abaddon informed me. "Elephants don't like anything small that moves quickly around their feet, but they're not terrified of mice. I'd call it an intense dislike. What elephants hate are bees. They'll flap their ears, make noises of distress and kick up dust when they hear the buzz of a hive."

I was silent as I stared at Abaddon. He stared right back. His poker face was incredible.

"Are you screwing with me?" I finally asked.

"I'd love to," he replied.

"Wait. What?" I asked.

"You heard me," he stated flatly. "But as far as mice and Demons go, I'm *not* screwing with you."

While I was pretty sure he'd just implied he wanted to bang me, I wasn't going to ask him to expound on it. My traitorous body was tingling, but banging wasn't in our future. The man didn't like me.

I was flustered, but had another important question. "Do Stella, Corny, Jonny, Moon or Irma know I'm Lilith's daughter?"

"As far as I'm aware, they don't. But one should never assume. They're not loyal to Lilith. They're loyal to no one," he said.

I nodded. Dagon had said the same. "Do you have any idea who the assassins are? Or how many of them will be involved in the game?"

His fists clenched at his sides and it looked like he wanted to do more property damage. "Unfortunately, I don't know the answer to either of your questions. Expect the worst and hope for the best."

"Not really helpful," I muttered. "But the truth is always better than lies."

"Speaking of the truth, my turn," he said.

"For what?"

"The word game," Abaddon informed me with a cagey glance. "I choose Truth or Dare."

"Dude, seriously?"

"Deadly," he replied coolly, waving his hand and repairing the broken table. "Pick your poison, Goddess Cecily."

I didn't want to choose either option, but I wasn't going to break my end of the deal. He'd given me a lot of good information. "Umm... truth."

"Do you have feelings for Slash Gordon?" he asked through clenched teeth.

Of all the things I thought he might ask, that wasn't one of them. "No. None."

He visibly relaxed. I visibly tensed.

"Choose," he insisted.

A dare was tricky especially with the direction he

seemed headed. I was wildly attracted to the Demon even though he had little regard for me. Abaddon was obviously still sexually attracted as well. Being intimate with someone I was in love with who didn't return the feelings would kill me as dead as Pandora's vicious game. It wasn't happening. "Truth."

"Are you in love with anyone?"

God, he was mean. I knew he was pissed that I'd broken the spell, but humiliating me was low. The only humane part was that he chose to shame me in private. If he needed to put me in my place, so be it. I was a badass, but even so, the payback was harsh… "Yes," I snapped. "He's a mean asshole and I plan to get over him soon. Hate kills love. Let's go with truth again, Dick. It's cathartic."

"Very thin line between love and hate," he commented. He looked like the cat who'd eaten the canary. If I had a mouse in my pocket, I would have thrown it at him and tested his desensitizing training. "Do you believe your spell worked?"

I rolled my eyes and made a disgusted noise. "Clearly it did if your gaping hole of ass behavior is any indication."

He paused for a long moment then dropped the bomb. "It didn't."

A feather could have knocked me over. My body acted of its own accord. I electrocuted the Demon. He laughed and slapped out the fire. I did it again. He reacted the same.

The third time was always the charm… I blasted him.

He didn't retaliate. He was far more mature than me. Not surprising. He was older than dirt.

After waving his hand and repairing the damage I'd

inflicted, he crossed his arms over his chest and went on as if he hadn't been on fire thirty seconds ago. "Fate is fate. No spell can alter it. You can't spell yourself out of being a Demon. I can't change the day I was born."

"You mean hatched," I muttered rudely.

"Semantics," he countered dryly.

I didn't have the luxury of losing focus. He was a shit for informing me right now. But two could play The Information I Don't Want game. "Fate may be set, but destiny is mine. I have no desire to attach myself to an ego maniacal jackhole. You're a heinous jerk. You blew up Sushi's club. At the studio you threatened me and treated me like dirt. You brought your fuck buddy with you when you were stalking me. You might have the compulsion to want me, but I have the control to say no."

He had the grace to look mortified. "I might have been a little mad," he admitted. "And Shiva is *not* my fuck buddy, as you so eloquently put it."

I slammed my fists on the table trying to crack it like he did. All I ended up doing was breaking my fingers. "Dammit," I shouted, looking at my quickly swelling hands. I held them up to the idiot. "This is your fault, Dick. And if your display of shittiness was you being just a *little mad*, then you need some anger management classes. Like a decade of them. We might be compelled to love each other, but I call big bullshit on that. I love coconut, but I'm allergic to it. I don't eat it. Same freaking principle."

"The compulsion isn't a magic bullet that makes me want you," he reminded me. His calm demeanor was infuriating. "All the compulsion accomplishes is helping one recognize what fate intended."

"Fate's a bigger dick than you are," I snapped. "Destiny is mine to shape and I don't want you in it."

He sat with that for a long moment. "Would it help if I apologized?"

My hands were aching. My head was pounding. "Nope."

"How about if I went to these anger management classes you seem so keen on?" he suggested, looking confused and uncomfortable.

It was clear that apologizing and compromising was out of his wheelhouse.

"Nope."

"Diamonds?"

I just glared at him. Buying me was the last thing that would work.

He was at a loss... probably for the first time in his life. "Begging? Flowers? Lemon trees? Twerking in a public place?"

My eyes widened and it was all I could do not to laugh. "You didn't just say you would twerk in public."

He became as alarmed as I was amused. "Fuck. Is that the one you're going to pick?"

I sighed and let my head fall back. The ceiling of the training room was cracked from our demolition. The bright pink and orange sunrise peeked through. It burned through the thin fractures in the metal like it was radioactive. It was a rude yet stunning reminder that I had a big and deadly evening ahead. Listening to Abaddon bargain for forgiveness wasn't on the agenda.

The truth was I wanted to bang the man like a screen door in a hurricane. I was perturbed with myself at how much I wanted to cave. In the past I'd been a loser in the love department. Was I willing to take that risk again?

Maybe.

Standing up, I looked the Demon straight in the eye. My heart beat like a jackhammer in my chest. I was an idiot. Whatever. I'd probably be dead tomorrow. "Slow," I said. "Slower than a snail. If you want to see if we'll work, we'll date. No nookie. No make-out sessions. It will be platonic until we *both* trust each other. You're a lot to handle and so am I."

His smile made him stupidly gorgeous. "I can work with that."

I eyed him and debated if I was going to tell him what I was thinking. I went with it.

"Do all Demon appendages grow back if removed?" I asked before I stated my other stipulation.

My question alarmed the Demon. I simply waited for the answer.

"Yes. Appendages grow back."

"All appendages?" I pressed, wanting to be confident before I made my threat.

"Yes. Why?" he asked warily.

"Because if I catch you with Shiva or any other woman, I'll castrate you," I informed him.

His laugh of delight made me think he was unhinged. "Wonderful," he shouted. "Same goes for you."

I winced. "I don't have a penis."

"Whatever," he said still gloating over my jealousy. "I'll just lock you in a cage until you come to your senses."

We were a match made in Hell… literally. However, a cage seemed much nicer than dismemberment. I had no plans to cheat. It wasn't how I rolled. Ever.

"Deal," I said, unable to bite back my grin.

His smile was wider than mine. I was probably the dumbest Demon alive, but I felt pretty damned good right now.

However, as good as I felt, there was a battle to be fought. "What will happen to Pandora when this is over?"

Abaddon's smile disappeared. "As soon as you free your father, all of Hell will rain down on Pandora."

I nodded. "I can work with that."

Abaddon walked around the table and stood in front of me. His scent made me dizzy and I was tempted to ignore the no nookie rule. If I was going to bite it, it was tragic that we hadn't done the deed.

From the gleam in his eyes, he was aware of my thoughts and agreed.

"Soon," he whispered. He took my swollen and broken hands in his. A swirl of sparkling red glitter covered our hands as the Demon healed me. "You will win. There's no alternative. I don't want to live in a world without you in it."

"No alternative," I whispered in agreement.

Putting his strong arm around my shoulders, he led me out of the destroyed training room. "You need to sleep for a few hours, Cecily."

I yawned. My stomach was full, but my body was lethargic. I didn't know the logistics of how I would get to Vegas, but knew Lilith, Dagon, Shiva and Abaddon would figure it out for me.

"Will you stay with me while I rest?"

The Demon I was dating pulled me closer. "Yes. There's nowhere in the Universe I'd rather be."

CHAPTER EIGHT

"HOLY SHIT," I GASPED OUT, HOLDING ONTO THE DASHBOARD in terror.

After my nap, we'd poofed from the cottage to a compound an hour away from the set where the game was to be played. I'd been outfitted with concealed weapons, another blood exchange with my mother and had the makeup Shiva had given me. From the compound it was decided we would drive. They would drop me off a half mile away and I would walk the rest of the way in.

Lilith was behind the wheel. I wasn't sure who thought that was a good idea. Candy Vargo was a crap driver. My mother made her look like a champion of safety on the road.

The car was some kind of SUV. It had three rows of seats and bullet proof glass. Dagon and Abaddon sat in the back. Lilith and I were in front. Shiva had gone to LA to back up Cher, Ophelia and Fifi in the protection of Sean.

Before she'd left, I'd removed the spell and given her Slash Gordon's digits. She was thrilled and had informed everyone of our newly minted and somewhat hostile best friend status.

I didn't correct her. It wasn't worth it. If she was happy, she'd protect my brother better. That was all I cared about.

Lilith was driving erratically and talking to me. Problem was, she looked right at me when she spoke and not at the road. My stomach was in my mouth. I figured if we crashed, we'd come out of it alive. However, showing up in Fake Vegas in pieces was a bad plan.

"Umm… do all Immortals drive like this?" I choked out as she narrowly missed clipping a truck.

"Like what?" Lilith asked, confused.

"Like batshit crazy?" I clarified.

Her laugh reminded me of tinkling bells. Despite the fact I was sure I was going to end up decapitated in a wreck, I laughed along with her. It was impossible not to catch her joy.

"I'd suggest we pull over," Abaddon said, feeling my impending freak out and backing me up.

Point for the Demon I was dating.

"Why?" Lilith asked as she almost slammed into the divider in the median due to the fact that she had fully turned around to address Abaddon.

"Because you're a horrible driver," I yelled as she veered back onto the highway and crossed all three lanes in one almost disastrous move.

"Oh my," Lilith said, flipping off an irate driver who was

fully within their rights to beep at us. "I don't drive much!" She punctuated her statement with another giggle.

Thankfully, she pulled over onto the shoulder.

"Better?" she asked with a twinkle in her eye.

"Much," I said, rolling down the window to get some fresh air so I didn't puke from the residual terror coursing through me from her death-defying driving. "Maybe, I should drive."

One would think people older than time would be good behind the wheel of a vehicle. One would be wrong. Very wrong. My guess was that Abaddon could drive since he spent a lot of time on this plane, but I could be mistaken. The preferred mode of transportation with Demons seemed to be poofing. Abaddon could be as bad or even worse than Lilith and Candy Vargo. Dagon was lovely and calm, but that didn't equate to good driving either.

"Do you actually have a driver's license?" I asked Lilith.

"A what?" she replied, confused.

I turned around and glared at the other two Demons in the car. "Do either of you have driver's licenses?"

"Legal driver's licenses?" Dagon inquired, totally serious.

Pressing my lips together so I didn't laugh, I shook my head. "I'm driving."

"Wonderful!" Lilith said, hopping out of the car and walking around to the passenger side.

Dagon leaned forward and patted my shoulder. "Thank you. That was quite brave."

"Brave?" I asked.

"Oh yes," he said with a chuckle. "Rarely does anyone let the Goddess know when she's not stellar at something."

I rolled my eyes and got out of the car. That was dumb. Lilith was a big girl. She could handle the truth. She was a shitty driver.

"Sorry about that," she said sheepishly. "I wanted to be your mom and drive you. I missed out on so much."

I sighed. "How about this?" I suggested. "If I live, I'll teach you how to drive."

Lilith fanned herself and started to cry. "Really? You would do that?"

"Umm... yes."

She wiped her tears and gave me a radiant smile. I was tempted to hug her, but didn't. I was moving slowly with both her and Abaddon.

"You will live," she said firmly.

From her mouth to whoever's ears... "Did you drive when you were pregnant with me?" I asked.

"Oh no." She shook her head. "Bill insisted he loved to drive and drove us always."

I bit back a laugh. My dad didn't love to drive at all. Clearly, he'd been aware of Lilith's appalling skills behind the wheel too.

As I moved to go around the car, Lilith stopped me with a hand on my arm. "Cecily, I'm not thrilled that you're going to play Pandora's game, but I know there's no stopping you. If the situation was reversed, I would do the same."

I nodded and waited for more. There was always more.

My mother cupped my cheek in her slim hand. It felt heavenly. "You're a Goddess by birthright. A true Goddess is a leader to all her people... even those who are not loyal to her."

I tilted my head and tried to suss out the hidden meaning of her words. "Would you like to tell me what you really mean by that?"

"I mean exactly what I said. Just because you don't understand it yet, doesn't mean it's not true."

Her words were similar to Candy Vargo's. Although, Candy's were more profane—*just because you don't understand something doesn't mean it's not fuckin' true.* The riddles the Immortals spoke in were enough to make me want to yank my hair out.

"Lilith, all the cryptic stuff is messing with my head. Is there any way you could be clearer?"

My mother grew pensive. She might be a piss poor driver, but she was a badass Goddess—true in every sense of the word. Her people worshiped her because she was fair and she gave of herself to them.

"The goal of the game is to save your father. It is against Demon law to harm a human, but Pandora doesn't care. Ignore her rules and make your own. Work from a place of compassion and love… it's the only thing that defeats evil. Take from what you know and use it even if it seems absurdly human. You have to stay alive to succeed."

So many thoughts raced through my mind. The given definition of Demon that I'd known was skewed. My mother seemed more angelic than demonic. Although, Cher had made it clear that Angels could be assholes. Confused didn't begin to cover the turmoil in my brain.

"Stop thinking, Cecily," Lilith said. "Sometimes trying to make sense of the nonsensical will hinder you. Let the answers reveal themselves. Nothing is black or white. Ever.

Demons are fallen Angels. Inside all of us is both good and evil. How we choose to mold our destiny controls which side wins out."

"That's a lot," I said with a slightly hysterical laugh.

"I agree," Lilith said in a serious tone that didn't chase away the butterflies in my stomach. "Let go of it and let your instincts guide you. Let your love for your father help you find your way."

"Okay," I said. "I can do that." My words were more confident than I felt, but I had to start somewhere. "Dagon said to look for signs."

The Goddess Lilith winked at me and smiled. "Yes. Look for the signs. They'll be there even if I can't be."

"Got it," I told her even though I didn't get it. Looking at my watch that doubled as a compass, I inhaled deeply. "We have to go."

FOR OVER TWENTY-FIVE MINUTES LILITH HAD BEEN TALKING nonstop. At least she wasn't behind the wheel.

"You're an excellent driver!" Lilith announced from the backseat.

Abaddon had moved to the front passenger seat. Having him next to me was calming. I didn't want to dissect it, so I didn't.

"Thank you," I told Lilith. "Is there anything else you guys can think of that isn't dripping in hidden meaning to tell me?"

Dagon leaned forward. From the rearview mirror, I

could see his glowing red eyes. "There will be cameras everywhere," he said. "Know that no conversation is private."

And the news kept getting worse.

"Has anything like this been done before?" I asked, feeling queasy.

"Pandora enjoys Demon hunts," Lilith said with a disgusted grunt. "She has staged hunts in the Darkness and had them televised through a network she controls."

"How is that allowed?" I demanded. It was every kind of psychotic.

"It's not allowed," Abaddon ground out. "However, there is little we can do. It's normally comprised of her people. They show their loyalty by dying for her."

"I can think of far better ways to be loyal," I mumbled.

"As can I," Lilith said flatly. "What her people choose to do with their free will is up to them."

"But this time it's not free will," I pointed out. "And the freak is supposed to be in time-out."

Lilith growled. It shook the entire car. "When Bill is safe, Pandora will suffer far more than a time-out. She's gone too far this time."

"Backup shall be waiting," Dagon assured me in a tone that made the hair on my arms stand up.

"Will Pandora be there… with my dad?"

"Most definitely," Lilith said. "Her ego wouldn't allow her not to be. She'll televise herself as well as the action the entire time. If you can find a monitor, you might be able to find her."

We drove in silence for a few more minutes. The good

thing is that I knew my way around a sound stage. I'd grown up on sets. I'd never had to literally fight for my life on them, but that was then... this was now.

Abaddon gently squeezed my shoulder. "Stop the car, Cecily. We've arrived at our destination."

They were the words I was waiting for yet didn't want to hear.

In the distance, the evening sky was lit up with neon lights and enormous roving spotlights. Around us was barren desert. The road in front of me was rutted and full of potholes. Walking it would be tricky, but it was the least of my worries.

"Everyone out," Lilith commanded.

The Goddess who stood in the middle of the desert was frighteningly stunning. Lilith glowed an iridescent silver and her eyes were glittering red. Abaddon and Dagon were no slouches themselves. The magic rolling off of them made it difficult to breathe.

"Repeat after me," Lilith said to me. "Close these walls and hide my secrets."

"Close these walls and hide my secrets," I said.

She nodded with satisfaction. "Do not use the spell often or Pandora will catch on and counteract it. When you need to speak without being spied on, use it quickly."

"Wait," I said, confused. "Spells don't have to rhyme?"

My mother looked at me like I'd lost it.

"No," she confirmed.

I noticed Abaddon trying not to smile. How was I supposed to know that?

"So, I don't have to address them to anyone in particular?" I pressed. "And say thank you at the end?"

Lilith was now seriously confused. "Umm... no."

"Well, that would have been handy to know," I muttered. I'd been pulling embarrassing verse out of my ass with my spells. "I just state what I want?"

"Correct," my mother said. "What have you been doing?"

"You don't want to know," I replied. "How do I end the spell?"

"State that it's done," she explained. "Or truly, you don't have to do anything."

My God, I'd gotten myself into a tizzy for nothing. "Just to confirm," I said, wanting to know if I'd been wrong about other things. "Spells won't work on Pandora."

"True," Dagon stated, still glowing like he was about to detonate. "However, they will work on those around her."

"Use caution," Lilith advised. "Pandora is a master spellcaster."

"Okay," I said, trying to put a list in order of importance together in my head. It was long and confusing. I felt a scream of frustration bubbling up in my throat.

Abaddon took my hand and looked into my eyes. His gaze was intense and kind of scary. "Get it out, Cecily. Now. Calm yourself before you go in."

I squeezed his hand hard. "Is an explosion okay?"

"Absolutely," Lilith chimed in. "Blow up the car. I don't like the color. It doesn't go well with my complexion."

The comment was so out of nowhere, I laughed. The SUV was blue. I didn't question her. The idea of blowing it to smithereens was too tempting. If she changed her mind, I might cry. Badasses didn't cry… or maybe they did. I just knew I needed a stress release and the SUV would do the trick.

"Will an explosion be noticed?" I asked before raising my hands high.

"Won't matter," Dagon said, pointing in the direction of the set of the game. "There are fires and explosives going off everywhere."

He was correct. It looked like a nuclear Fourth of July.

"Back up," I instructed. The last thing I wanted to do was to harm anyone I cared about.

The sound of the metal ripping apart at the seams and the fire that accompanied was thrilling. I squealed with delight at the melting steel and rubber and watched as it morphed into a smoldering pile of goo. My body relaxed and I pictured Man-mom's face in my mind. He was my goal. I was ready.

"I can do this," I announced.

"And I need to do this," Abaddon said, pulling me into his arms and laying a kiss on my lips that made my head spin. As our lips met, tingle didn't describe the wild rush of pleasure that shot through me. It was intense, gentle, searching and mind-blowing all at the same time. His full lips moved against mine with promise and desire. My palms splayed against his chest as he wrapped his arms around me, holding me against his strong body and drawing me deeper into the kiss. My toes curled as I gave in completely. I didn't care that my mother and Dagon were watching. Actually, if they hadn't been, I would have been tempted to rip the man's clothes off. The timing was bad, but the need was real.

"Sorry, not sorry," he said with a lopsided grin on his face as he pulled back.

I was still hanging onto him since my knees felt like jelly. "I take back the no kissing rule," I whispered with a grin bigger than his.

"Works for me," he said. "Don't die. I'll be furious if you do."

"Roger that, Dick," I said with a laugh. "I have no plans to die." I glanced over at Lilith then back at him. "Suddenly I have a lot to live for."

CHAPTER NINE

THE HALF-MILE-WALK DOWN THE DARK ROAD FELT SHORT. Leaving Abaddon, Dagon and my mother behind felt like I'd ripped off an appendage and forgotten it. However, I knew in my heart I was walking in the right direction.

There was an ivy-covered arched gate at the entrance to the set where the deadly game was to be played. No one was there. The town was lit up like neon on steroids. It seemed deserted. I knew full well it wasn't. Strangely, I saw none of the other players. Maybe, that had been bullshit as well. Maybe, I was the only one playing the game.

The town was not large. That wasn't to my advantage. From the looks of it, it consisted of three roads about a quarter of a mile each. Different sized buildings lined each street—tall and short. Neon signs and billboards were everywhere advertising sex, drugs, gambling and weapons.

"Nice," I muttered. "Classy."

Quickly, getting out of the middle of the street so I

wasn't a sitting duck for an assassin, I made my way into the fake town along the exteriors of the buildings. I'd done a few films where I was running from the bad guys. Granted, they weren't Demon assassins, but Lilith had insisted to pull from what I knew. I definitely knew that standing out in the open wasn't going to end well... for me.

I found it interesting that the cameras weren't well hidden. There were several on each building and on all the street signs and billboards. There were no camera men or women. All the equipment had been set up and was running on its own. That was stupid. I could jam every single camera with a quick spell. Not that I would... Man-mom was the goal. Infuriating Pandora wasn't the first order of business.

The buildings I passed felt solid. Lots of times sets were made out of plywood and cardboard. This was brick and steel. I wasn't sure if the buildings were facades or fully built structures. There was only one way to find out.

Glancing around, I tried to guess which one would be safest... as if any of them were safe. I was standing next to a strip club. On the outside chance it was a real strip club, I kept walking. There was a pawn shop, a check cashing store, a massage parlor, and an escort service. None of them were appealing.

"Bitch," someone whispered from a doorway a few feet ahead. "We're in here."

It was PT Bitch aka Irma Stoutwagon. I was shocked she was being helpful, but then realized it might be a trap. The goal, as far as they knew, was to be the last Demon standing. If Irma was offing the competitors so she could win, I might be walking into a trap.

"Show me the others," I demanded, ready to pull out a lipstick and incapacitate her for twenty-four hours. The irony that the move would probably save her life wasn't lost on me. Honestly, I felt bad they were involved in this hot deadly mess. Pandora wanted my head on a platter and they might die because of that.

Irma stepped back and one by one the others quickly popped out then back in. Stella Stevens, Corny Crackers, Jonny Jones and Moon Sunny Swartz were with PT Bitch. The gang was all here.

Keeping the lipstick handy, I made my way over and slipped inside. The building was a fully realized peepshow house. Thankfully, no one was performing. It was empty other than us. I cased the medium sized room. I spotted only three cameras out in the open. My guess was that they were the only ones if the sloppy camera locations outside were anything to go by. Pandora was so full of herself she didn't seem to believe in stealth. Win for me... hopefully.

Without being too obvious, I indicated the cameras in the room to the others. The only one who didn't appear surprised by the intrusion was Jonny Jones. I reminded myself, the idiot wasn't as stupid as he wanted us to think.

"Close these walls and hide my secrets," I said.

The cameras hissed and sparked. All five players gaped at me in shock. I really looked at each of them. They were probably going to die at the expense of Pandora wanting me six feet under. That was wrong. My mother's words danced in my head—*a true Goddess is a leader to all her people... even those who are not loyal to her.*

I wasn't exactly the Goddess in charge and these nightmares weren't loyal to me. Why in the hell did I feel a responsibility to them?

"What the fuck are you?" Moon demanded.

"Cakehole. Shut it," I said. "We probably have about two minutes before they figure out the cameras shorted out." Lilith said to make my own rules. I was all over it. The longer I could keep them safe, the better. "As far as picking allies, I say we round robin it. That way if one of us dies, their partner doesn't."

"Quite daring," Corny said. "I like it."

"The other thing is that none of us are leaving here alive if Pandora has her way. We're simply entertainment for her followers."

"Where are you getting your information?" Stella ground out.

"Honestly, I'm guessing. She wants me dead. All of you are unimportant collateral damage."

"Fuck you," Irma snarled. "I am not unimportant."

The cameras began to magically reform.

"Listen to me," I snapped, cutting Irma off before she went on a tirade that included bloodshed. "We're about to stage a fight with each other."

They perked up at the suggestion of violence. "We're not going to truly maim or harm each other. What we need to do is break the cameras. If they think we're stupid enough to off each other without the assassins getting involved the better for Pandora—less blood on her evil hands."

Everyone was perplexed and wary.

The cameras began to hum quietly again. If they weren't

going to follow my lead, I was about to go down in flames. Hopefully, they weren't all idiots.

"Corny, you son of a bitch," I yelled, taking a swing at him and knocking out camera number one. "I had to do years of therapy after you exposed your wrinkly raisins to me when I was a kid. I should kill you for that!"

It was a little much, but it spurred my posse of assholes into action.

"Fuck that," Irma Stoutwagon shrieked. "Moon Shitass Swartz pranked me and I lost a huge endorsement deal. It was for Vagisil! I was set to make the big bucks off of the vagina cream, but that cow bitch banged the ad execs and told them that I used Monistat and smack talked Vagisil. I will never forgive you for that!"

My mouth was wide open, both from the story she'd just shared and the violent way she picked up Moon Sunny Swartz and hurled her into one of the cameras. Irma gave me a quick thumbs up as Moon lay in a bloody heap on the floor.

They took their *fake* violence very seriously.

"And you," Jonny Jones shouted at a still gloating Irma. "You stole my dancing shoes at the audition for *So You Think You Can Dance*. I stuck to the floor during my turns because of you. I could have been a star!"

Irma threw her hands in the air. "I don't know what you're talking about, dick cheese. I've never auditioned for that."

Jonny didn't care. He sprinted across the room and dropkicked Irma into the third camera.

"Dude," she shouted as she hopped up and wailed on him. "I call bullshit. You lied."

"I'm a Demon. Sue me," he said, wiping the blood from his face where Irma got an excellent right hook in.

They both started laughing. Holy hell, these people were nuts.

"Cameras are out," I said. "No more pummeling each other."

"Why is Pandora after you?" Corny Crackers questioned.

"Not important," I said. "Just know that she is, and I'm not guessing on that."

Moon came to and joined us. "I thought the contract was screwy."

"It's bullshit," Jonny said with a sour expression. "I only took it because of the death threats."

"Same," Irma chimed in. "So, what's the plan? Kill Pandora?"

I wanted to say yes so badly, I could taste it. I didn't. "No. The goal is to save the human man, Bill Bloom."

"Because?" Stella asked.

The truth was easier to remember than lies. "He's my father."

"That is utter crap," Corny announced, pointing a bony finger at me. "You're a Demon. You have a purple fire sword which means you're an *old* Demon. There's no way that a human man is your father."

I inhaled deeply then exhaled slowly. A chilly wind blew through the room as I wiggled my fingers. I felt the slight burn in my eyes and knew they'd turned red. When my body began to glow, they all took a healthy step back. My actions and appearance unnerved them.

"I'm forty. Bill Bloom is my father. My mother is a Demon. I'm getting my dad back from Pandora even if I have to die doing it. I don't like any of you, but I want you to understand what you're up against. The game is a death wish. I'd suggest you leave now."

"And let you be the star of the show?" Irma demanded.

I squinted at her. "Are you insane? Did you hear anything I just said? I'm trying to save you from a sure death."

"I heard you," she snapped with a triumphant expression on her face.

She was missing brain cells. Maybe all those cartwheels had knocked her good sense loose.

Irma wasn't done. She was more batshit than I'd originally thought. "Word on the street is that you have a new TV show. Rumor has it that it's going to be a huge hit."

I didn't have time for this crap. "Your point?"

"You want your dad back?" she inquired.

"Stupid question," I said.

She shrugged. "You can't do it alone. You need us."

I wasn't sure where she was going with her line of warped reasoning, but the others were following her discombobulated train of thought and were in agreement.

With what? I had no clue.

"I'm giving you an *out* so you can live to see tomorrow," I reminded all of them.

"And I'm giving you an *in* to save your precious father,"

Irma shot right back. "As long as you're willing to give a little something in return."

I winced. It became frighteningly obvious where the conversation was headed.

"Yes, yes," Corny said, flapping his hands in excitement. "I'd be willing to stay and aid you for a recurring part on your new TV show!"

"Fuck to the yes," Moon bellowed. "My insurance just ran out. I could use a new gig."

"I too could use a good vehicle to stretch my thespian chops," Jonny Jones commented.

This chat had taken a turn into Oh-Fuck-No Land.

"I'm still very hot in Hollywood," Stella Stevens told us. "My tits are legendary."

Everyone rolled their eyes, me included.

"Screw all of you assholes," she hissed. "You would be lucky to have me on your little show, Cecily Bloom. So, my answer is yes! I will stay and help for a role on the show."

All eyes were on me. Sean was going to tie my ass in a knot if he had to write for these talent-free freaks. But... if we were using my past humiliating showbiz stories, the people in this room fit right in. Perfectly. We'd use the reality angle for real...

"Deal," I said, even though I knew I'd live to regret it. However, I had a better chance of living and rescuing my dad if they were my small and very dysfunctional army. "Season one only. If you don't suck, we'll discuss season two."

The cheers were loud. It was strange to see such joy considering the situation we were in. However, I'd take a little happy wherever I could get it. The cameras were still down.

"Okay." I motioned them all to gather in close. "Pandora can't know we've joined forces. Each of you have powers that will be useful."

Irma looked perturbed. "What do you mean by that?"

I didn't blame her for her fear. If she was a known mouse shifter to the Demon population, she wouldn't last five minutes. I wasn't going to out her, but I wanted to be clear I knew.

"Stella, you're an excellent backstabber who can sense danger," I said, pointing at her.

"Guilty," she squealed with a delighted giggle.

It was a little difficult to gauge her expression since she'd done so much Botox, but the giggle was a positive sign she wasn't about to punch me.

"Jonny, you can go invisible and are much smarter than you let on," I continued.

Jonny gave everyone his mega-watt smile and took a bow.

"Corny, you're a pervert who can fly," I said.

"Bingo," he said, grabbing his wrinkled junk with pride. I was relieved he was wearing clothes.

"Moon," I went on. "You have zero fear of repercussion which is quite obvious from the bullshit stunts you've pulled on sets."

"Thank you," she said.

"It wasn't a compliment."

"Whoops, my bad," Moon said.

"I should say so," Irma muttered, still obviously put out about the Vagisil deal.

"Moving on," I said, before they had a smackdown over it. "I also know Moon can attract danger by humming."

"Correct," she replied, flipping Irma off.

I pointed at Irma. "Your given name is Irma Stoutwagon."

She gasped and paled.

"You're vicious in battle and have a special skill that we will only use if necessary."

Her relief that I didn't let the cat… or the mouse out of the bag was huge.

"What are you?" Irma asked the same question that had already been asked.

I shook my head. Telling them I was a Goddess wasn't in the plan unless I had no other choice. "I'm a badass and Pandora's worst nightmare."

"I can work with that," Moon said. "Oh, and just a reminder, there are twelve assassins. Two for each of us."

"How do you know that?" I asked.

She gave me a weird look. "Didn't you read your contract, dumbass? It was in the fine print."

"Not in mine," Jonny Jones said.

"Or mine," I added. "Quickly, each of you tell me something pertinent you found in the fine print. My guess is we all had different contracts."

"I didn't read it," Stella said.

"No fucking surprise there," Irma commented.

"Mine said the award's ceremony would take place in the castle on the set," Corny shared.

Again, that was news. It was good news. If the castle was the end point, that meant Pandora was probably there.

"Has anyone seen a castle?" I questioned.

The short answer was no. It wasn't wise to wander around looking for it, but that was exactly what I planned to do. I felt it in my bones that Man-mom was there. Avoiding the assassins while searching for the castle was on the new agenda.

"In my opinion, the cameras are a problem," Jonny Jones pointed out.

He was right. I paced the room and slapped together a plan in my head that hopefully we'd all survive.

"Let me get something straight," I said before I laid out the scheme I'd just yanked out of my ass. "All of you are willing to stay and help me knowing you could die to be on a TV show?"

"Absolutely!" Corny Crackers assured me as the others nodded enthusiastically.

The things an actor would do for work…

"Alrighty then, here's the plan until it's not," I said. "On my command, we'll exit the building. Goal is to find the castle and not bite it."

"Liking it so far," Stella said. "Especially the not biting it part."

I kept talking. "Corny, fly above the cameras and stay out of sight. Be ready to dive in and fight when it gets ugly. Jonny, you go invisible and hide Irma and Stella behind you. That will obscure them. Stay close to the wall and near enough to me to back me up when the assassins attack."

"Exciting!" Jonny said, shivering with delight.

"How many of you have purple fire swords?" I asked.

No one raised their hands. My stomach dropped.

"No worries," I lied, worried out of my mind. How were they going to defend themselves? Whatever. We'd figure it out as we went.

"What about me?" Moon asked. "Want me to pull a prank?"

In unison, everyone yelled NO.

"You're with me," I explained. "When I tell you, you'll hum and draw them to us. We stand a better chance that way."

"Won't they see our every move on the livestream?" Jonny inquired.

He was not dumb at all. "Nope. I'm going to cast a spell to short out all the cameras. There's a chance if Pandora isn't in control, we could draw her out. We can make it look like an accident. Is anyone good at starting raging infernos?"

"Hell to the yes!" Moon volunteered. "I can also fart into the fire and it will freaking explode."

No one commented on that. If she wanted to literally risk her ass, that was on her. Irma raised her hand.

"Yes?"

"I know it's already been asked, but what the fuck are you?"

"I'm a forty-year-old former child star who happens to be a Demon with a few extra perks," I supplied. "I'm here to save my dad and make sure Pandora eats shit."

"I like your style, bitch," Irma announced.

"Thank you," I replied. "Note to all. If we can get all

twelve assassins together at the same time, I think I can take them."

"How?" Corny Crackers asked.

I smiled and raised my hands in the air. Not only one purple fire sword appeared, but two.

The applause was loud. I took a bow and prayed to a shitload of stuff I didn't believe in. However, the one thing I believed in was me.

Dread necessity was one hell of a motivator.

CHAPTER TEN

IT WAS TOO DAMNED QUIET. THE FEELING OF MICE
skittering up my spine made me shiver. Why hadn't the
assassins shown up yet? Moon's contract had said there
were twelve. That didn't mean it was accurate. Demons lied.
However, Pandora was in her territory and felt safe. I'd been
shocked at how lax security had been when we'd gone after
Abaddon at her casino. It would be true to form if she didn't
have the set of her show heavily guarded. Her arrogance
was astounding. Crossing my fingers hard, I sent positive
vibes into the Universe that the evil woman's ego would
bring on her downfall.

Corny had stripped down to his tighty-whities, exited out
the back of the peepshow business and flown high above the
town. He'd insisted it was easier to fly without the hindrance
of clothes. I was simply relieved he left his grundies on.
Jonny snapped his fingers and went invisible. The faint scent
of rotten eggs was detectible. Abaddon had gotten his facts

right. That didn't surprise me. The Demon I was *dating* didn't miss much. Stella and Irma got behind Jonny. I couldn't see any of them. It was perfect. They slipped out of the building and hid in an alley two doors down.

It was Moon Sunny Swartz's and my turn.

"You ready to go out there?" I asked her.

"Born ready, Cecily Bloom," she replied.

The bizarre woman was a handful. I wondered what had happened in her life that made her so stupidly reckless. People's stories always fascinated me. I had a feeling hers might be tragic.

"Moon, how old are you?"

She eyed me warily then shrugged. "Seven thousand give or take a few hundred years," she replied.

Wrapping my head around the number was hard. The thought of living forever was a foreign concept. How did people not lose their minds? Half of the time I felt old at forty…

Was I going to live forever? As a half-human/half-Demon, I wasn't sure. Although, it had been implied by a few that I had a long life ahead. I could potentially outlive everyone I knew. Well, not everyone, but Sean and Man-mom for sure. The thought of missing them for eternity was unsettling. I shook the feeling off and focused on the now. My dad could not die today. I wasn't anywhere near ready to mourn him yet.

"Can I ask another kind of strange question?" I inquired.

"I got nothing to hide," she told me.

I doubted that. "Did you know Stella, Irma, Jonny and

Corny before this?" I was aware she knew Irma because of the Vagisil debacle, but I was curious about the others.

"Oh yeah," Moon said. "We're in a knitting club for Demons—the Yarn Yankers."

A light wind could have blown me off my feet. She had to be pranking me. "I'm sorry. What?"

"The Yarn Yankers," she confirmed. "I'm known for my baby booties and blankets. I donate them to a homeless shelter."

She had to be full of it, but her face told me nothing. "Seriously?" I pressed.

"As a fucking heart attack," she promised. "That shitass, Corny, knits teddy bears, hats and schlong warmers."

That somehow rang true.

"Jonny?"

"Specializes in muffs, if you know what I mean," she informed me waggling her eyebrows.

I did know what she meant and it was nasty. I moved on. "Stella?"

"Heart shaped knitted ice packs to use after plastic surgery," Moon said.

Again, that one made sense.

"Irma?"

"Leg warmers," she supplied. "Ugly as fuck."

"You're not pulling my leg?" I asked, realizing I'd made a crappy pun, but still finding the club hard to swallow.

"Nope, not this time. Do you knit, Cecily Bloom?"

"No, I don't," I said quickly. If by some chance the club was real, I wanted nothing to do with it. Although, learning more about the idiot posse I'd acquired made me want to protect them even more.

"That's too bad. It's a good time. We knit then beat the daylights out of each other. Oh, and Cecily, before we go out there and potentially eat shit, I'd like to apologize for humping and orgasming on the furniture of that TV show we did back in the day."

"Umm... okay."

"Yeah, that wasn't my finest moment," she admitted, while miming humping. "You might not have noticed, but I have a little issue with impulse control."

Little was an understatement, but I didn't voice my opinion. Opinions were like assholes... everyone had one and more often than not it was rude to show it.

"Well, everyone has their off moments," I said, trying to be diplomatic since she seemed to have a heck of a lot of them.

"Right," she said with a smile. "I'm getting better about reining it in. My therapist is the bomb."

"That's terrific, Moon."

"Thanks," she replied. "But you have to admit, that set furniture was really sexy. Gave me a big lady-boner."

Again, with the mimed humping.

At a loss for words, I wasn't sure how to react to her admission. I pressed my lips together so I didn't say anything terrible. I knew fully well my eyes had widened and my expression was pained.

"Got ya!" she shouted with a laugh.

Groaning, I laughed. I wasn't entirely sure she'd been exaggerating about her attraction to the sofa and love seat, but I wanted to end the discussion. Now. Moon Sunny Swartz was a piece of work. "Yep, you got me."

"So, do we have a plan when the assassins show up?" she asked, cracking her knuckles and doing a few more humping motions.

"Off them before they off us," I told her. "Once they're eliminated, we storm the castle. But first you set a fire and I jam all the cameras."

"Love it!" she shouted.

I hoped her mode of fighting didn't involve humping. If it did, I'd soon find out. She'd been alive for seven thousand years. The Demon must be able to defend herself. "Let's get this party started," I said, using the phrase I used with my friends at home.

"Roger that," she said. "Let's make like a baby and head out!"

"Or that."

Moon was socially unacceptable and had a major lack of impulse control, but for some weird reason, I liked her. I made a mental note of the line, *let's make like a baby and head out*. It was awful, but I had a feeling if used in the right scene, it could get a laugh.

I was always up for a good cheap laugh.

IT HAD BEEN QUIET INSIDE THE PEEPSHOW BUILDING, BUT outside it was eerily silent. I detected Jonny by his faint rotten egg scent behind me. Covertly glancing up, I noticed Corny Crackers had removed his underpants. I didn't have a problem with nudity. My Uncle Joe had been a nudist when he was alive and was still naked as the day he was born in his ghostly form. However, seeing Corny's wrinkled junk again after being beyond grossed out by it all those years ago was unappetizing.

"Whatever works," I muttered, scanning the street and the windows of the buildings. "Where are they?"

"Don't know, but this is as creepy as fuck," Moon whispered, glancing around warily. "I feel like a hunted animal."

"Pretty sure that's the point," I reminded her. "Before you hum, I have one more quick question."

"Shoot," she said.

"Can you guys actually fight?"

She looked at me like I was as nuts as I thought she was. Moon Sunny Swartz threw her head back and cackled like a loon.

"Dude," she said, shaking her head. "You ain't seen nothing until you've seen the Yarn Yankers in battle."

I hoped to Heaven, Hell and everywhere in between she wasn't overexaggerating.

I took a deep breath and exhaled on a woosh. "Hum, Moon. Lemme see how good the Yarn Yankers really are."

"You have a preference?" she inquired.

As I considered my choices, I landed on one and grinned. "How about a little AC/DC? Hell's Bells works for me." The irony of the choice didn't escape me. Plus, my brother, Sean, could literally teach a college course on everything AC/DC. He would heartily approve.

Moon chuckled. She snapped her fingers and produced a huge gong and a mallet.

"Is that necessary?" I asked.

"If you want Hell's Bells it would be a fuck show not to get the opening correct," she informed me. "Do it right or don't do it at all."

I gave her a thumbs up. Sean would agree. "Do it right. And start the fire."

Moon spit in the wind and a raging inferno began to burn. I was amazed that she was skilled enough to keep it from coming at us. The nutbag gave me a thumbs up. I gave her one right back.

As she hit the gong, I felt the sensation vibrate through my body and down to my toes. All of a sudden everything became very real. We were about to face twelve flaming assholes with our deaths on their agenda. I needed all six of us to come out of it alive. When Moon started to hum, I felt the pull to my Demon side. My body began to glow as the scene in front of me was washed in scarlet. My eyes were spitting ruby sparks, and I was ready to rumble.

"I'm coming, Man-mom," I whispered. "Hang on for me. I'll be there soon." It was time for the spell. "I wish for the cameras to be destroyed."

They hissed and shorted out.

The flaming Demon assholes arrived only seconds after Moon began to hum. They looked the same as the others who'd tried to kill me. This time, like the last time, I had no plans to die.

It was to our advantage that they seemed confused. The lure of Moon's humming had thrown them off. Instead of hiding themselves and picking us off, they were out in the open.

There were twelve of them and six of us. The disgusting assassins with goat eyes were literally on fire—green fire with icy-blue sparks flying off their enormous bodies. They stood well over six feet tall and were all bulging with grotesque muscle. The searing heat that arrived with the assholes rivaled Moon's fire as they walked right through it. It made me feel lightheaded and sick to my stomach. The putrid smell of sulfur wafted in the air.

I would have given anything if this was a dream. It wasn't.

Pulling the eyelash curlers from my pockets, I hurled them at the enemy. I was aware it wouldn't kill them, but it would buy a little time.

The biggest one, who I guessed to be the leader of the bunch, bellowed with rage. It shook the ground. "All of you will die." His voice sounded like he'd chewed up and swallowed broken glass. "Take the Goddess alive for Pandora. She wants the honors of ending the abomination."

"Quick question," Moon said as she pulled throwing stars and some glowing daggers from her pockets. "Are you the Goddess that the soon to be dead fucker is referring to?"

"Yes. Is that a problem?"

"Nope. Just getting it straight," she said then ran at the flaming assholes like a bomb out of a cannon.

I screamed. She was going to freaking die.

The fire that covered the assassin's bodies sparked and grew hotter. I felt rooted to the ground. Sweat poured down my face. What the hell was Moon thinking? They went at her like they were starving and she was a perfectly cooked medium rare steak.

"Not today, Satan," Corny Crackers shrieked as he dive-bombed the evil Demons with what looked like knitting needles in his hands. I was so alarmed at the weapon he'd chosen I didn't even flinch that his junk was flapping in the wind.

"This is a shitshow," I shouted. Pulling on my magic, I produced my purple fire swords and began lopping off heads before my little posse got decimated.

Since the orders included keeping me alive, they didn't come at me. However, they were all over my dysfunctional army. Moon was missing an arm, but she somehow bare-handedly beheaded an assassin with her remaining appendage.

Point for the Yarn Yankers.

As I fought my way over to Corny, I watched in horror and awe as he used freaking knitting needles to remove one of the more aggressive Demon's heads. The blood and gore were stomach churning, but the move was disgustingly impressive.

"I'm coming to save the day!" Jonny Jones shouted as he, Irma and Stella sprinted out from the alley.

Jonny, no longer invisible, didn't look a thing like the Jonny I knew. The strange man was a monster. Abaddon clearly hadn't been aware of Jonny's extra talents. He had to be over eight feet tall and had claws and fangs that would live in my nightmares for years to come.

He also wasn't fucking around.

When he opened his jaw, his head appeared to detach. It was insane. In one single move, Jonny Jones bit the heads off of three wildly shocked Demons. He spit them out then went for more.

"How many left?" Stella yelled over the roar of the fire and the ear-splitting growls of the assassins.

"Six. One for each of us!" Moon yelled back.

"Look at these," Stella Steven's shouted as she marched into the middle of the street.

She was topless and her silicone enhanced rack was bouncing spastically. As her left breast bounced up the right went down. She wiggled her rear end and her boobs swung in circles—the left went right and the right went left. It was nuts. The flaming assholes were clearly boob men. They were entranced. Demons were horny bastards.

Stella had been correct earlier. Her tits were legendary. However, she hadn't told the entire story of her bosom. As the assassins were locked on to her weirdly talented tits, she clapped her hands.

My mouth dropped open as sharp objects began to fly from her nipples. The blades were like heat seeking missiles and flew right at the flaming assholes. The one in the front got the worst of it. The metal embedded in his neck and began to magically saw his head right off his body.

That definitely broke the boob spell the assassins were under. They charged Stella with murder on their minds. Of course, in any good script, the naked dude comes to the rescue of the damsel in distress who can massacre with her mammaries. Corny flew in, scooped up Stella and propped her on top of a billboard with an ad for Viagra. It was all kinds of weirdly appropriate.

However, there were five bastards left.

With a scream so high pitched it shattered the windows in the buildings on the street, Irma Stoutwagon joined the melee. She reminded me of a rabid Tasmanian Devil on crack... or maybe a pissed off honey badger on a week-long cocaine bender. She was out of control. Even Jonny Jones in monster form took a wary step back.

The flaming assholes didn't stand a chance. Irma worked fast and violently. The speed at which she moved rendered her invisible for brief moments. It seemed likely all of us would suffer hearing damage from her piercing screams. The blood, guts and body parts that flew everywhere made the bile rise in my throat. The need to hurl was real. I was down with beheading evil Demons who wanted me dead, but Irma took it to another level.

I was pretty sure I'd been hit in the head by a blood-soaked kidney, but didn't want to verify it. Irma's rampage was so vicious it made the bloodiest Hollywood horror flick look like a G rated kid's movie. When she was done, there was very little recognizable of the five flaming assholes she'd shredded limb from limb.

"And that's how it's done, bitches," Irma announced as she drop-kicked what was left of one of the assassin's heads.

Moon spit in the wind and put out the fire she'd created. "Dude," she shouted, slapping Irma on the back with the hand she had left. The other arm was already growing back but was just a stump. "That was insane."

"Thank you," Irma replied, taking a bow.

The others gathered around Irma and congratulated her. I stood on the outside of the circle still flabbergasted from what I'd just witnessed.

"Hey, Goddess," Moon said. "Join in. We won!"

I nodded absently and walked over to the crazy group. All eyes were on me.

"Do you have something you'd like to share?" Corny inquired with a raised brow.

I kept my eyes on his face since he was still in the buff. "I do."

"By all means, start talking," Stella insisted, crossing her arms over her ample and dangerous chest.

At least she'd had the wherewithal to put her top back on. At another time I would ask her how she did the boob thing. Or maybe not... Some things were better left a mystery. However, I owed them the truth. "Corny, put some clothes on. Your junk is making me gag."

"I've got this," Jonny announced, no longer in monster form.

He waved his hand and dressed us. Since we were covered in gore, it was a nice thing to do. His taste was crap. He'd chosen western-wear complete with cowboy hats, enormous silver belt buckles and boots. Whatever. At least it wasn't covered in blood.

I cleared my throat and began. "Well, first off, thank you for fighting the assassins. That was umm..."

"Mind-blowing?" Corny offered.

"Fucking awesome?" Irma added.

"Orgasm inducing?" Moon chimed in.

"The first two, yes. The last one, no," I said. I took a deep breath. It was fact that they pledged their loyalty to neither of the Goddesses. It was anyone's guess how the news of my heritage was going to sit with them. Stuffing my hands into my pockets, I was relieved that the lipsticks and the tooth-picks from Candy Vargo were still there. I didn't know how, but I wasn't going to look a gift horse, or a monster in Jonny's case, in the mouth. If it went sideways, I could knock them out for twenty-four hours and get on with saving my dad.

"Start talking, Cecily Bloom," Irma said. "If that's actually your name, bitch."

"It is," I told her. "My name is Cecily Bloom. I'm the daughter of the human Bill Bloom and the Goddess Lilith."

"Holy shit," Moon yelled.

"How old are you?" Jonny demanded.

"Forty."

That left all of them silent.

I kept going. If they wanted to leave after the rest of the story, I'd still let them do the TV show. They'd made my life a whole lot easier with their horrifying fighting prow-ess. "I didn't know my mother was my mother until very recently. I didn't even know I was a Demon until very recently."

"Yet you have two purple fire swords?" Stella asked with doubt written all over her mostly frozen face.

"Correct. The Grim Reaper taught me how to control my power and the Demon known as the Destroyer helped me as well."

"Ohhhhhhh, Abaddon," Moon said with a swoony sigh. "I'd bang that hottie in a heartbeat."

My eyes narrowed to slits and my hands began to spark. My batshit violent army backed up. "He's mine," I said flatly.

I was sure Abaddon would be delighted to hear me claim

him. My territorialism made me feel a little icky, but if I was laying it out, I would lay all of it out.

"Roger that," Moon said, saluting me. "Lots of other psychotic fish in the sea."

"Back to my story," I stated. "Needless to say, my existence gives Lilith the upper hand. Pandora doesn't like that. She's been trying to kill me for a while."

"Bitch hasn't succeeded," Irma pointed out. "Good on you."

I gave her a tight smile. "She kidnapped my father. She wants me to trade myself for him."

"Are you planning on doing that?" Corny asked, concerned.

I ran my hands through my hair and looked up into the night sky. It was starless and cloudy. "I love my dad. I'm going to get him to safety no matter what I have to do," I answered honestly. "I feel it in my gut that Pandora and my dad are in the castle somewhere around here. I'm going to find it and them. Once I do, I'll pull the rest out of my ass."

"In my opinion, the best laid plans are always pulled from the ass," Jonny assured me. "My ass is full of outstanding plans."

"Or expelled from the ass," Moon added.

I smiled. The Demons were bizarre. "I think you should all go home. It's going to get ugly fast—uglier than the battle with the flaming assholes. My promise that you'll be on the show stands. You helped me get rid of the assassins. That was huge and I thank you again."

The five exchanged cryptic glances. One by one, with Irma Stoutwagon going first, they got down on their knees before me. It made me uncomfortable and want to laugh at the same time. All I could see was the top of their cowboy hats.

"Get up," I instructed. "I'm not really a working Goddess so to speak. I barely know how to be a Demon."

"Bullshit," Moon yelled. "You're a badass. It's written all over you. I've never seen anyone with two fire swords and you lop heads off like you've been doing it for centuries."

I knew it was a compliment, but I had a hard time thanking her. In my struggle accepting who I was, I didn't love the super violent part.

"Fuck to the yes," Irma added. "I'm not one for Demon politics—too violent for me."

I choked back a laugh. Irma was the most violent Demon I'd come across so far.

"But," she continued. "It's getting tiresome being rogue. I'd be down with pledging my loyalty to a bitch like Cecily Bloom."

"I quite agree," Corny said. "Plus, let us not forget that if Cecily dies there is no show."

Horrified murmurs came from all.

"In my opinion," Jonny chimed in. "It's best that we do a blood oath. It's permanent and that means Goddess Cecily will protect us."

I winced. "I'm not real sure you guys need protection. You seemed pretty damn good in battle."

"It's more than just protection," Stella explained. She sighed dramatically. "We used to be loyal to that shitty whore Pandora several thousand years ago. It wasn't a good time."

"Underfuckingstatement," Irma said. "We were allowed to leave as long as we didn't pledge our loyalty to the Goddess Lilith."

"Correct," Jonny Jones said. "However, now that there's a new Goddess in town, we wouldn't be breaking the oath with the shitty whore."

"Guys, I'm barely a Demon, much less a real Goddess," I protested.

"Blood doesn't lie," Moon said. "You're the daughter of a Goddess, therefore you are a Goddess. And the bonus is that you're not the daughter of the shitty whore."

I pressed my temples. It didn't seem like there was any easy way out of this. Although, I was totally down with calling Pandora a shitty whore.

"Listen, bitch," Irma said, fiddling with her belt buckle. "We've spent thousands of years without a community to call our own. We have to fight off Demons from both the shitty whore's side and Lilith's side. It fucking sucks."

"Word," Moon agreed.

"The ladies—and I use the term loosely—are correct," Corny said, sounding older than time. "I know for a fact we were chosen for this game because no one would care if we live or die."

That made my heart hurt. "I'm not even sure I'm allowed to have followers."

"Don't be obtuse. You're a Goddess," Stella pointed out.

"I am. However, I've barely been to the Darkness."

"No biggie," Stella said. "We don't go to the Darkness— too dangerous for people like us. We're the expendable ones."

Stella's statement pissed me off. No one was expendable. "I feel woefully underqualified and under-rehearsed to be responsible for anyone. I don't even own a cat."

"I call bullshit, again," Moon said. "You walked in to this shitshow and told us to leave so we wouldn't die. That's Goddess talk. You're telling us to leave again... which we're not going to do by the way. You keep trying to save us. That's Goddess talk. All you have to do is a blood exchange and we're yours."

I squinted at her. "I don't want to own people."

"Even better, bitch," Irma said. "We don't want to be owned. We want to be part of something larger than the Yarn Yankers. It's pretty simple. You accept us and we have your back. Not fucking complicated."

It *was* fucking complicated—very complicated. I scanned the faces of the whack jobs who wanted me to be their Goddess. Each of them looked so hopeful, it made me waver. It would be hilariously fitting that I might be in charge of the misfits.

They were not loyal to the shitty whore. They were not allowed to be loyal to Lilith. I wouldn't be poaching anyone's people. If I had to be a Goddess I might as well use it to help. It didn't look like there was any way out of being a Goddess except death.

I wasn't down with dying yet.

"How does a blood oath work?" I asked.

"Easy peasy," Moon said, pulling out one of the glowing daggers that she hadn't used in the battle. "A little slice, a little slap of hands and done."

"That's it?" I asked warily. Demons tended to leave out pertinent details.

"That's it, bitch," Irma said, grabbing Moon's dagger and slicing her own hand.

Time was ticking. My head and heart told me it was the right thing to do to take them under my wing. I just hoped it didn't mean we'd be hanging out together a whole bunch. They were a pain in the ass.

Irma held the dagger out. I took it and sliced my own palm. The second I began to bleed my entire body glowed silver and the air around me grew thick with magic. Shimmering crystals in every color of the rainbow danced around me and my crazy crew.

"Holy shit," Jonny Jones muttered with a wide smile.

"Amazing," Stella Stevens agreed, taking the dagger and slicing her hand.

One by one, I slapped hands and exchanged blood with the five Demons who had just saved my ass. One by one they dropped to the ground to show their respect. With each of the exchanges, my magic increased. It was scary and welcome. I hoped to hell and back this didn't mean I would end up fighting like Irma or have to be naked to fly like Corny. And I really hoped it didn't mean my boobs were now weapons or that I could morph into a monster with a detachable head. Although, if it would save Man-mom, I'd embrace it. I'd just need a lot more therapy to deal with it.

Corny Crackers was the first to speak. The old geezer had tears in his eyes. "I pledge my loyalty to the Goddess Cecily. From this day forward I am at your service. In your presence, I vow to keep my junk covered for the most part."

I swallowed my laugh. The man was serious.

"In my opinion," Jonny Jones added, "this is the most exciting day of my fifty-thousand years. The bonus is that Cecily isn't a shitty whore."

"Word," Stella Stevens said, curtsying to me. "My tits and I are your loyal subjects until we bite it."

If someone had told me I'd be gaining a batshit crazy posse for eternity this evening, I would have freaked out. However, the reality of it was strangely moving.

Moon Sunny Swartz gave me a thumbs up and a bow. "I'm all in for worshiping the Goddess Cecily. For you, I promise to work on my impulse control and will not perform any pranks on the set of your new hit show."

That was a tall order for Moon, but I didn't comment. The fact that she was willing to make an effort was good.

Irma Stoutwagon made everyone's bows look paltry compared to hers. She slowly slid into the splits while bobbing her head. I was worried she'd split the crotch of her jeans. Miraculously she didn't.

"I pledge my allegiance to the bitch Goddess Cecily," she announced. "I will do irreversible damage to anyone who fucks with her—including the shitty whore. And just so you know… the Yarn Yankers are aware of my special skill and don't fear it."

My brows shot up in surprise. "Really?"

"Yes," Corny said with a sour expression. "Irma trapped us in a cage and shapeshifted so many times it desensitized us."

Jonny paled to the point I thought he was going to faint. "Yes. It was not a pleasant decade."

"Wow," I said. I wondered if that was what Abaddon, the Grim Reaper, Dagon and my mother had done as well. It seemed harsh, but whatever works...

"Shall we find the castle, save Bill Bloom and deal with the shitty whore?" Corny inquired, clearly wanting to move on from the ten years in a cage.

"Yes," I said. "Yes, we shall."

CHAPTER ELEVEN

"IT SHOULDN'T BE THIS DIFFICULT TO FIND A DAMN CASTLE," I muttered as we walked the streets of the small town while keeping our eye out for more assassins. The contract had said twelve. We'd taken care of that problem. However, Pandora wasn't known for playing fair. The town was lit up like Christmas. The neon billboards glowed so bright it made my head pound. They seemed to be mocking me.

"No shit, Sherlock," Moon said in frustration.

We'd been searching for the castle for a good forty minutes. Fake Vegas wasn't large, and really it was as far from Vegas as a wanna-be Fake Vegas could be. I didn't dwell on it though. I had bigger Demons to fry. As small as the place was, finding a castle didn't seem like it would be that hard. I was wrong. My little army and I had combed the streets multiple times. Nothing. Moon had humped a fire hydrant hoping it would bring good luck. It hadn't. Corny had offered to fly around and see if the castle was possibly hidden in between the buildings. I'd said yes. Unfortunately, he had to strip down to his birthday suit to get the job done. I hadn't cared. That's how desperate I was. Sadly, he hadn't found anything that looked remotely like a castle.

He opted to stay naked just in case he needed to fly again.

Dagon had said to look for signs. Lilith had backed up his statement. I took it as a sign that Corny, Stella, Jonny, Moon and Irma were with me. But that was a reach. I kept expecting to hear a whisper in my head with directions or something helpful.

So far, nothing.

I'd also been encouraged to use what I knew. Candy Vargo had said to pull from what I know and wing the rest. I was an actor. It didn't seem helpful.

"Let's take cover and brainstorm," Jonny suggested. "Maybe a few acting exercises will help."

En masse we slipped into a pawn shop. It was just an empty room. Stella snapped her fingers and a table and six chairs appeared. When Moon moved to hump her chair, Irma decked her. I was glad she did it and not me. Jonny's suggestion to pretend to be our spirit animals to find our centers was shot down unanimously.

"Define castle," Corny said, ignoring the fact that Moon was bleeding profusely.

I was pleased he was seated and the table covered his privates. Looking at his junk was not my idea of fun.

"Castle," Moon said, adjusting her nose that Irma had just broken. Thankfully, her other arm had grown back and she was able to realign her nose with both hands and a sickening pop. "According to the dictionary, it's a large building, typically of the medieval period. Usually fortified against attack with thick walls, battlements, towers and in many cases a moat."

"There's no castle here," I said, pressing my temples and wondering how to proceed. "If that's the definition, there's definitely not a castle on this set."

"We're looking for the wrong thing, bitch Goddess Cecily," Irma said.

I didn't comment on my title. I actually kind of liked it. "Keep talking."

She shrugged. "That's all I've got."

Use what I know… What did I know? What was I good at besides pretending to be other people? A slow smile spread across my lips.

"Word games," I said aloud. "It's a game. This entire shitshow is a game being played at our expense. It's time to turn the tables."

"You go, bitch," Irma said with a grunt of approval.

"Anagrams for castle," I said.

Corny reached under the table and came back up with a pad of paper and a pen. He slid it across the table.

I sucked on my bottom lip for a moment as I stared at the office supplies. I wasn't sure where he'd pulled them from and hoped it wasn't his ass. "Umm… where did you find that, Corny?"

He had the grace to look embarrassed. "My butt," he whispered. "Is that a problem?"

"Actually, yes," I told him. "It's lovely that you want to

help, but items literally pulled from your ass are not going to work."

He nodded thoughtfully. "I can see how that might be unappealing."

"Oh, for fucks sake," Irma grumbled, smacking Corny in the head then wiggling her fingers.

A nice, new pad and pen appeared before me with no fecal matter on it. Corny sheepishly took back the items he'd offered and reached under the table again. I was fairly sure he shoved them back up his ass, but didn't want to know.

"Cleats," Stella said. "Cleats is an anagram for castle."

"Eclats," Jonny added.

"What does that mean?" I asked, staring at the words I'd written down. I was too old to pretend I knew things when I had no clue. Granted, at forty I was a baby compared to the company I was keeping...

"Easy," Moon chimed in. "It means ostentatious display or dazzling effect."

"Use it in a sentence," Corny suggested, confused.

It felt kind of like we were participating in a spelling bee with a life-or-death trophy on the table for the winner.

Moon stood up and cleared her throat. "When Moon Sunny Swartz farted into the campfire on the retreat, it exploded and incinerated the entire forest. Her prowess with ass gas was received with great eclat."

"Mmkay," I said. "Not sure we're going in the right direction."

"Synonyms for castle," Stella suggested. "I'll start. Fortress."

"Stronghold or tower," Jonny said.

"Palace or possibly mansion," Corny added.

"Estate or manse," Irma said, flipping everyone off.

As crazy as it was, my gut said to go with Irma's answers. Since there wasn't much more to go on, I decided to trust my gut and her middle finger.

"Anagrams for estate," I called out.

"Tea set," Stella guessed. "They might be in a tea shop."

"No tea shops in the town," Jonny reminded her.

"Correct, but it was a good guess," I said, then moved to the next word. "Anagrams for manse."

"Names," Moon said.

"Mensa," Corny volunteered.

I stared hard at the word. The letters elevated off the paper and rearranged themselves. We all gasped as they reconfigured into a new word.

Amens.

It was a sign. It was cryptic, but that was to be expected.

"Amens?" Irma asked, confused. "What the fuck does that mean?"

Moon who was apparently a walking dictionary answered. "It's a word uttered at the end of a prayer or hymn, meaning 'so be it'. And full disclosure, even the mention of a prayer gives me gas. You might not want to be downwind of me."

We all moved.

"Did anyone spot a church in town?" I asked.

The laughter was uproarious. I took that as a no. We were dealing with Demons after all.

"Anagram for church," I instructed.

We came up with a blank on that one.

"Go deeper," Stella suggested.

I nodded and began to jot down whatever came into my head. "Priest, cathedral, mosque."

This was going nowhere fast. I let my forehead hit the table with a thud. We were too close to be this far away.

"Maybe we're wrong. Maybe Pandora isn't here at all," I whispered, trying not to cry or scream.

"Bullshit," Irma ground out. "The shitty whore is always where the action is. We just have to put on our fucking thinking caps and figure it out."

"I believe the foulmouthed Irma is onto something," Corny said. "The shitty whore is a game player. She always was and leopards can't change their spots."

"Agreed." Stella backed Corny up. "The shitty whore always sticks around until she's in danger. Then she sacrifices her own to get away."

I'd seen her do that. It had been horrifying.

There was no time for a pity party. Man-mom needed me. Candy Vargo said I was a badass. It was time to prove her correct. Glancing down at the three words I'd written down I went with them. Fate was set. Destiny was mine to mold. I was going to mold the heck out of it.

"Anagrams for priest," I challenged my people.

"Stripe," Jonny said.

I wrote it down. "Cathedral?"

"Umm… how about La Cathead?" Moon guessed.

I wrinkled my nose, but wrote it down. "Mosque?"

Irma laughed. "Mouse minus the q, bitches."

Corny, Jonny, Stella and Moon blanched, but none went screaming from the room.

"Oh, my goodness!" Corny gasped out as he levitated into the air. "I think I've got it."

His nuts were at eye level but I didn't care. "What?" I demanded.

"The Striped Pussy Lounge," he said. His entire body quivered with excitement. And I mean his entire body.

"Holy shit," Moon shouted. "I saw that storefront two streets over. It had a sign in the window that said no mice allowed. I thought that was weird."

I felt light headed. Excitement mixed with dread shot through my body. "That's where we're going."

My people cheered. I joined them.

"Wait! More info," I said, stopping everyone from sprinting out of the pawn shop. "Pandora is supposed to be in time-out for a decade. She got put there by the Keeper of Fate then escaped. Once I have my dad back safely, all of Hell is going to rain down on her."

"Will the shitty whore get put back in the box?" Stella asked with a shudder.

I tilted my head. "Is Pandora's box a real thing?"

"It is," Jonny whispered, glancing around to make sure no one but us was within earshot.

"Have you seen it?" I asked, also in a whisper. When in Rome…

"No," he said.

"Then how do you know it's real?" I asked.

He shook his head. "I don't."

"I think it might be metaphorical," Corny added unhelpfully.

Lilith said any box would do. It was the key that was important. I didn't have a key.

"Alrighty then," I said, changing the subject. "We're going to go with what we know and treat this like a movie. We're on a set, we may as well use it."

"Exciting," Corny sang, doing a full body shimmy.

I closed my eyes. "Someone dress him please."

"On it," Moon said, snapping her fingers and clothing Corny in a mumu. "Easier for him to rip off if he needs to fly."

"Love it," Corny assured her.

"In my opinion," Jonny began with his overused phrase. "It's not a real set unless there are cameras."

He had a point. Plus, the fact that if it really was being televised to the Demons, Lilith and Abaddon would be able to see what was going on if I fixed the cameras. "I can repair them."

"Rad, bitch," Irma said. "The camera loves me."

"Back to the plan," I said with the tiniest eyeroll I could get away with. "I'm the director. We're all the actors in the scene. Is anyone good at improv?"

"I'm outstanding at improv," Moon claimed.

The others nodded enthusiastically.

"Great," I said, hoping their improv was as good as their fighting skills. I glanced around to gauge who I trusted the most. I was surprised that it was all of them. Who knew? "Who wants to volunteer to bring my dad back to my home in LA once we get him from Pandora?"

"I shall do it!" Corny said, bowing deeply to me. "It would be my honor to transport the father of my Goddess to safety."

I smiled at the Demon in the mumu. "Thank you." I wrote down my address and handed it to him. "Do you know Ophelia?"

"Oh yes," he said. "Everyone knows Ophelia. She's a legend."

I chuckled. "Yes, she is. She's there along with a few others who are protecting my brother. You'll tell her I arranged for you to return my dad."

He bowed again, memorized the address then ate the paper. "Don't want it to get into the wrong hands."

I appreciated the gesture. I'd eaten my mother's calling card for the same reason. "Shit," I muttered. "There's a ward around my home."

"Here, bitch," Irma said, handing me a cell phone. "Call Ophelia and tell her to break it."

"She can't," I said, "but I know someone who can."

My mother had created it. She could break it. I tried to call Lilith. It wouldn't go through. My stomach roiled.

"Try texting," Stella said, looking over my shoulder. "The shitty whore is way behind the times. Figures she would block phone calls but she's too stupid to think about texts."

I texted my mother and made the request. I got a thumbs up and six happy face emojis in return. It made me smile. "Done." I also quickly let her know the cameras would be in working order shortly and to watch for when Man-mom was safe and the backup could arrive. That elicited ten more smiley faces.

"Are we ready to rumble?" Moon shouted.

I put my hand out. My crazy-ass people put their hands on top of mine.

"On three, we go! One," I said.

"Two, bitch," Irma yelled.

"Three," we shouted in unison.

We were ready to rumble.

CHAPTER TWELVE

"IT WAS RIGHT HERE," MOON SAID, SCRATCHING HER HEAD IN confusion. "I'm sure of it."

We were not standing in front of the Striped Pussy Lounge. We were standing in front of a massage parlor called Beat the Meat. I wondered who in their right mind named these businesses, but then reminded myself that Pandora's casino had been called Golden Showers Bet and Bed. The horrible woman was guilty of many things, but good taste wasn't one of them.

The clouds had cleared, but the sky was still starless. Only an eerie sliver of moon looked down on us. The air felt thick with desperation... mine. To give my little army credit, they were on edge as well, but I had far more to lose than they did. Magic, while useful, also sucked. This movie couldn't turn out to be a horror film. I needed a happily-ever-after action flick in a big way.

"In my opinion, you've humped too many objects and have lost brain cells," Jonny told Moon.

Moon growled. "Well, in my opinion, you should be tossed into an industrial fan set on extra high, jackass."

Stella walked over to Moon and Jonny and knocked their heads together. The sound was awful. "Act your age, not your IQ," she huffed. "Both of you."

"Stop," I said. "Maybe, Moon just got the street wrong. The town's not big. We can find it. In every decent script, the good guys never find the objective on the first try."

"That's correct!" Corny announced grandly. "Good things come in threes like comedy and triplets. I'm a triplet."

"You are?" I asked, kind of terrified of three naked versions of Corny Crackers.

"Oh yes," he assured me. "My brothers are realtors in Alaska. Nice fellas, quite violent. I'm the oldest. Beefy Crackers came a minute after my arrival then Sandwich Crackers was the third out of the hole."

I didn't know what to say so I kept my mouth shut. Demon triplets were a lot to swallow. Especially ones who were basically named after a corned beef sandwich. It was glaringly obvious what their mother craved while pregnant...

"I'd swear to the Darkness that the Striped Pussy Lounge was here," Moon insisted, nursing the lump on her forehead from the noggin knock.

"The shitty whore is screwing with us," Irma said with a scowl. "She's moving it around to make it more difficult."

I looked at Irma askance. "Can she do that?"

Irma rolled her eyes. "Of course, she's a shitty whore. That's what she does. She makes everyone's lives miserable."

"Crap," I muttered. "Where in the heck are the signs Lilith told me to look for?"

Corny gasped dramatically and began to levitate. Irma pulled him out of the air by his foot. "Signs as in sign-signs?" he inquired.

I squinted at him. He was missing some gray matter as well. "I was told to look for signs."

"*At* signs or *for* signs?" he pressed, getting excited.

"Does that matter?" I asked.

"Listen to me now," he insisted. "Believe me later."

I threw my hands in the air. My fingers itched to blow something up. My stress was at an all-time high. "I can't remember if it was to look *at* signs or look *for* signs."

"Not to worry," Corny assured me. "Over there." He pointed to a trio of lit-up billboards. "Tell me what you see?"

Stella answered before I could. "Ads for limp erections, prosthetic legs and naked yoga."

That wasn't what I saw. My entire body tingled, and I grabbed Corny so I wouldn't fall to the ground. The signs were there, and they were literal... very literal.

"Oh my God," I gasped out.

"God has nothing to do with this," Jonny said. "He's more of a concept than an actual being. I'd suggest something more realistic along the lines of 'Oh my Hell', or 'Slap my ass and call me Sally'. More appropriate for Demons. 'Holy shit' is acceptable, but I prefer, 'What the fuck?'"

I ignored him. While he might be smarter than he let on, he was still an idiot.

"What do you see, my wonderful bitch Goddess Cecily?" Corny asked, bouncing on his toes.

It looked like Irma's title for me was rubbing off on the others.

"First one says, *keep*. Second says, *going*. Third says, *right*," I wheezed out, still feeling wobbly and lightheaded.

"I don't see that," Stella said with a huff.

"That's because you're not a bitch Goddess like Cecily Bloom," Irma told her.

"What are we waiting for?" Moon shouted. "Turn right and haul ass."

We did.

"Keep looking for more signs!" Corny insisted as we took every available right.

"There!" Jonny yelled, pointing to the Striped Pussy Lounge.

It was five businesses down. When we got there it disappeared in a blast of shimmering black mist.

"Motherfucker," Irma bellowed.

I whipped around and looked for another sign. None of the billboards were talking to me. "There's nothing there except an ad for vaping."

"Not just the billboards," Corny said, ripping his mumu off in his excitement. "You said signs. Not billboards—which, of course, are signs—but they're not the only signs!"

I hugged the Demon. I didn't care that his junk was swaying in the wind. Although, I studiously avoided coming into contact with it.

"Brilliant," I told him as he blushed a deep red.

I changed my objective and began frantically looking at

street signs and storefront windows. "What's the name of the street we're on?"

"Evil Avenue," Moon said.

I grinned. The sign I saw was labeled, *Entrance* Avenue. "Go to the entrance of the town. Now."

We sprinted like the metaphorical devil was on our heels. The Striped Pussy Lounge was right where the sign had told me it was. And again, it disappeared in a gust of black mist when we got close. I didn't waste a moment on being pissed off. Hide and Seek wasn't a game I loved, but it was one I planned to win.

As I searched the signs in the area, I grabbed the still-naked Corny by the arm and gestured for Jonny to come close. Stella, Irma and Moon quickly joined us. I leaned in and whispered since the cameras were rolling. I barely moved my mouth so no one in the control booth could read our lips. "Okay, guys and gals, the third time's going to be the charm. Jonny, go invisible. Corny, you'll fly Jonny to the next location of the Striped Pussy Lounge. Stay behind him so you'll both be obscured. I think she's moving it the minute she sees us approach. If she can't see the approach, we can get in."

"Did something happen to your mouth?" Stella asked, concerned. "You sound like I did when I got a triple dose of lip filler and couldn't talk right for weeks."

I blew out a frustrated breath. "No. My mouth is fine. I'm trying to make sure no one watching the feed can lip-read what I'm saying."

"That's genius," Stella said, patting me on the back. "Next

time I overdo the lip enhancement that's the excuse I'm going to use."

"Glad to be of service. Are we clear on the plan?" I asked my nutbag followers.

They all nodded.

"I am so glad you're just a bitch and not a shitty whore," Jonny announced, bowing to me.

"Umm... thanks," I replied with a wince. A compliment was a compliment no matter how freaking insulting. "Get inside the door and hold it open for us."

"It's a brilliant plot twist in the movie," Corny gushed. "I think we'll be nominated for an Oscar!"

I refrained from reminding him this wasn't a real movie. I didn't want to burst his bubble. It was more of a life-or-death situation. Scanning every sign I could see, my eyes landed on a neon storefront sign. "Don't be stupid, look for Cupid," I read aloud.

"The matchmaking service—Cupid's Gigolos and Hoes," Stella said under her breath. "It's next to the peepshow house where we first met up. The Striped Pussy Lounge must be next to it now."

"Oh, my Hell, with these names," I muttered. I nodded to Jonny and Corny. They took their silent direction seamlessly. The gals and I hung back as Corny flew he and Jonny like a bat out of Hell. "I really hope they don't crash."

"That would suck ass," Irma agreed.

Holding my breath, I counted to three. "Go!"

I wasn't as fast as my newly found friends. Didn't matter. They pulled me along. At the speed we were moving, I was sure we'd disappeared from sight. That was definitely to our advantage.

Right before we dove through the open door of the Striped Pussy Lounge, I spotted one more sign. It said, *I believe in you.*

I groaned as I landed on the bottom of the Demon heap at the entrance of the castle that wasn't a castle at all. Sadly, Corny's junk was smashed against my ear. I extricated myself without wracking the Demon. I felt like that was incredibly considerate since I was beyond gacked out. Most of our cowboy hats didn't make it through the pileup. That was fine by me. They were heinous.

"We did it, bitches!" Irma hissed as she helped everyone to their feet.

We had, but there was another confounding puzzle in front of us. The outside of the building made it look like a single-story business. It was an optical illusion. Inside it was enormous—a ten-story-high vaulted ceiling with a maze of crisscrossing steel girders and enough doors and hallways to make me want to lose my mind.

"Unbelievable," Stella snapped, slapping her hands onto her hips. "What do we do now? I don't see any signs in here."

She was correct. The high-sheen marble floors and the shiny walls were blood red and the place was bare of any furniture or decor…. The message was clear. This was a trap and we were not supposed to come out of it alive.

"Alright, bitches," Irma said pacing back and forth. "I say we split up and search."

"You're stupider than you look," Moon grumbled. "This

place is a labyrinth. What happens if we find the shitty whore and can't find our way back?"

"Splitting up is the fastest way to find the shitty whore," Jonny Jones pointed out. "We could be weeks in here and find no one."

"It's tragic we didn't think to bring long-range walkie-talkies," Moon said.

I looked over at her. "Can't you just magic some up?"

She tried... and failed.

Corny tried.

Stella tried.

Jonny tried.

Irma tried.

I tried.

We all failed.

"The shitty whore cast a spell in here to dampen magic," Irma ground out. She punched one of the blood-red walls and it punched her back. Her eye swelled shut immediately.

"Well slap my ass and call me Sally," Jonny Jones screamed, moving away from the walls.

"This is a freakshow horror house," Moon cried out, humping the air around her.

"I think the walls have ears," Corny whispered. "And fists."

He was correct. Without a word, Irma shoved us all together into a tight circle. She spoke at a barely audible volume. "Pig Latin."

"I'm sorry, what?" I asked, sure I'd heard her wrong.

"Pig Latin," she repeated. "When we wanted to say something that the shitty whore couldn't understand, we spoke in Pig Latin."

"She's right," Stella confirmed. "Hetay Hittysay ohoreway siay upidsay. Andorapay ancay ebay ooledfay."

"I didn't understand that," I told her.

"I said the shitty whore is stupid. Pandora can be fooled." Not gonna work," I told her. "Too complicated."

"You're not fluent in Pig Latin, bitch?" Irma asked, surprised. "Didn't speak it as a kid to mess with your dad?"

"Nope," I admitted, ready to electrocute all of them. "Also, I don't think splitting up is the way to go. We need to protect each other."

"Goddess talk," Moon said with a nod of approval.

"Crap," I said, looking down at my hands. "Did Pandora take my magic with her spell?" I was tempted to test if my purple fire swords were still there but didn't want her to know what I could do in case the freaking walls had eyes as well.

"A Goddess can't steal another Goddess's power," Corny whispered.

I stared at all of them for a long beat. "But I'm kind of a junior Goddess."

"Give me a break, bitch," Irma said with a grunt of disgust. "I traded blood with the shitty whore thousands of years ago. Her blood is nowhere as powerful as the shit you slapped on us earlier."

"Really?" I asked.

Moon leaned in. "And then some."

"But I couldn't magic up walkie-talkies," I reminded my rag tag bunch.

"That takes practice," Stella informed me. "Hang on a sec. Let me try something."

She whipped off her shirt and did her boob dance. It was mesmerizing in a terrible way. I was glad she didn't shoot heat-seeking missiles out of her nipples. There was no telling what the walls would have done to us.

"Magic is fine. The shitty whore has just blocked communication instruments," Stella confirmed, putting her shirt back on.

I gave her a tight smile. "Great. But if the walls have ears, we really do have a problem. Or... maybe not."

Everyone looked at me expectantly. I wasn't sure it would work. Lilith could communicate with her people telepathically as a Goddess. I was a Goddess. The whackos staring at me were my people. It was worth a shot.

"Testing. Testing. One. Two. Three. Can you hear me?" I asked silently.

"Yessssss, bitch!" Irma hissed with delight.

"Oh my!" Corny said with his hands clasped together. "Wonderful."

My relief was overwhelming. I could still direct the movie. So far, so good. However, the costumes weren't working for me. We looked like idiots.

"We need to look badass," I told them.

"On it," Jonny said.

Stella kneed him in the nuts before he had a second go at dressing us. He'd struck out the first time. She wiggled her pinkies and the cowboy duds disappeared. Other than Corny, who she dressed in a mumu again for ease of getting naked to fly, the rest of us were in all black—black combat pants, black long-sleeved t-shirts and black shit-kickers. It was perfect.

I quickly checked my pockets to see if the lipsticks and toothpicks were still there. They were. I wasn't sure how the Demons did that but was grateful. Fiddling around, I realized I had six tubes—enough for all.

"I'm giving all of you a tube of lipstick," I explained as I pulled them out of my pocket.

"I love makeup!" Corny gushed.

"It's not real lipstick," I warned. *"It's a weapon—a laser. If you point and squeeze at your enemy, you'll incapacitate him or her for twenty-four hours."*

"Are you shitting me?" Irma asked, admiring the tube before tucking it into her pocket.

"I shit you not," I said. *"I'm not sure what kind of protection Pandora has, but this might come in handy."*

Moon raised her hand.

"Yes?"

"I'd prefer we call her the shitty whore," she said.

I laughed. *"I can work with that. Remember, the goal is my dad's safety. Period. The shitty whore will be dealt with by Immortals way more powerful than all of us put together. Got it?"*

"Roger, bitch Goddess Cecily," Jonny said with a salute.

"So," Stella said, glancing over at the plethora of doors and hallways. "Which one are we going to take first?"

Lilith's words came to mind as I stared in consternation at the problem before us—*let go of it and let your instincts guide you. Let your love for your father help you find your way.*

Growing up, Man-mom had always insisted that in order to make a wish on a star come true, you had to turn around three times before you wished. I still did it to this day and I was about to do it again.

I closed my eyes, turned around three times then opened them. The first door my eyes landed on was the one we were going to walk through.

"That one," I said.

Hopefully, the luck of the stars was on my side.

CHAPTER THIRTEEN

THE HALLWAYS WERE A MAZE. FOR OVER AN HOUR WE'D RUN around like hamsters on a wheel going nowhere fast. Twice we ended up back where we'd started. Each time we believed we'd made ground we were back at the beginning. We took great care in staying away from the walls. It was crazy, but they seemed hungry. They undulated and trembled as we sped down the corridors.

"This is absurd," Stella griped.

"I do believe we're missing something," Corny announced.

"Ya think?" Irma grunted, pacing in a circle and dropping F-bombs.

Moon humped the air in frustration. "We're lost. This place is huge."

I agreed with everything they'd said, including Irma's F-bombs. We stood in a random hallway that looked identical to the other hallways we'd been down. I wasn't giving up.

Ever. It was another game Pandora was playing with us. There had to be a way to win it and get to the prize. I refused to believe otherwise. The soft mechanical hum of cameras sent my Spidey senses into overdrive.

"Does anyone see a camera?" I asked, looking around. I could hear them but couldn't spot them.

My people shook their heads.

Crap.

It was time for a quick spell. I had no intention of shorting out the cameras, but wanted conformation they were here and that I wasn't imagining it. The cameras meant that the shitty whore could see us, but it also meant that Abaddon, Dagon and Lilith could as well.

I summoned my magic and commanded, "Show me the cameras."

In less time than it took to inhale, hundreds of small high-tech cameras oozed out of the blood-red walls. It was creepy and the sound was disgusting.

"Dude," Moon whispered with a laugh. "That sounded like a shart."

Corny was perplexed. "A shart?"

"A shit fart," Moon explained.

"Ah yes, of course," he replied.

The second-grade humor mixed in with the dire situation was a bizarre stress relief. A pained laugh quashed my need to blow something up. The Demons with me were my people—for better or worse. Right now, it was for the better. Even though I was only forty, I felt motherly toward the dumb-dumbs. The thought of harm coming to them made my stomach tighten.

The hum of the cameras grew louder now that they were exposed.

If there were cameras—and there definitely were, someone was controlling them. Pandora wasn't hip to technology according to Stella. The lack of her blocking texts was the proof. It was a logical guess to believe someone else was running the technical side. The question was, how many and where were they?

Again, my mother's advice danced in my head. When I'd asked for more clarification on Pandora, Lilith had been convinced she would be present at the game. The shitty whore's ego was so massive, she would also be televising herself out to the Demon audience. My mom had said if I could find a monitor, I might be able to find Pandora.

In a skyscraper full of endless doors and hallways, it was something to go on. We'd had very little luck so far.

"New plan," I said. "We're going to find the control room for the cameras. I think it will give us a better idea where the shitty whore is hiding."

"How will we find the ontrolcay oomray?" Jonny asked in Pig Latin

For once, I understood him clearly. "We're going to pull that part out of our asses."

"Excellent hinkingtay," he said with a salute.

"Gather close," I instructed. My mind raced and with that came discombobulated ideas, but stopping to consider the pros and cons wasn't on the agenda. "Put Irma in the middle. Everyone, squat down and hide her completely from the lens of the cameras."

They did as told.

"Irma, I want you to shapeshift. I'll carry you in my pocket. When we get to the control room. I'll let you do your thing. I need you to clear the room of flaming assholes."

My posse paled, but Irma grinned like a fool.

"My pleasure, bitch Goddess Cecily."

In a small poof of pink glitter, she went from Irma the batshit crazy Demon warrior to Irma the batshit crazy adorable brown fuzzy mouse. The craziest part was that she could still talk. It was freaky. Corny, Stella, Jonny and Moon gagged a little, but didn't lose their debatably sane minds.

While Irma could still speak, she sounded like she'd swallowed a vat of helium. "Okay bitch," she squeaked. "Put me in your pocket and let's have some fucking fun!"

I gently picked her up and tucked her safely into my pocket. *"Don't mess with the lipstick or the toothpicks,"* I warned her.

"Roger that, bitch," she said in her new and arguably cute voice. It was funny to hear a mouse swear.

"Okay troops," I said, smiling at my friends. *"Do you guys have any more talents I don't know about yet?"*

"But of course," Corny shared. "Jonny is an expert hacker. He's stolen billions from banks. Very impressive."

"Thank you," Jonny said, feigning humbleness.

I blew out a frustrated breath. We were going to have a sit-down and talk about right and wrong if we made it out of here alive.

Corny wasn't done. "As you already know, Stella can sense danger and kill with her knockers, but she also hunts by scent on all fours like a bloodhound."

"Is that true?" I asked her. The mental picture was disturbing.

"Totally," she confirmed. "It's hell on my knees, but my ass looks amazing when I'm on all fours."

"It really does," Jonny added.

"Agreed," Corny chimed in. "Moon, as you are aware, can start infernos with saliva and attracts danger by humming. She's also a nationally renowned square dancer."

I forced myself not to laugh. *"Square dancer?"*

"Yep," Moon said with a devious grin. "With a twist."

Did I dare to ask… I did. *"Twist?"*

Irma piped up from my pocket. "Do NOT square dance with the bitch. It's like *The Red Shoes*. If you start dancing with her, you'll do-si-do until you drop dead."

"Bullshit," I said in disbelief.

"It's not the do-si-do that's the problem," Moon corrected the talkative mouse in my pocket. "It's the allemande left or the roll away to the right sashay that kills."

I wasn't sure if I was being pranked or not, but I made a mental note never to square dance with Moon. Although, the image of a bunch of flaming assholes rolling away to the right sashay until they were no more was wildly satisfying.

"Corny, do you have any more secret powers up your mumu sleeves?" I asked. Knowledge was power. Or in the case of Moon, it was confusing and alarming.

"Why yes I do," he said with a naughty grin.

I held my breath and waited.

"I can find the source of energy and suss out mechanical issues," he let me know.

"Not following," I said.

"Let me explain for the old bastard," Moon chimed in. "When Irma loses her phone, which is all the fucking time... Corny can touch her charger and find her phone. Or if your garbage disposal gets clogged because Jonny the jackass put a gallon of coleslaw down it, Corny can touch the on/off button and let you know exactly where the pipe is clogged."

"Correct," Stella said. "And if your car is making terrible sounds, Corny can touch your key and tell you what the problem is."

"I can," Corny agreed. "However, you wouldn't have problems if you occasionally put motor oil in your vehicle."

"Or gas," Irma shouted from my pocket.

"Wait," I said, getting excited. *"If you touch one of the cameras, could you tell us where the control room is?"*

"Oh my!" Corny said, hopping to his feet. "I do believe I could!"

Could it really be this easy?

In a flash, Corny sprinted over to the wall and touched the cameras with both hands. His scream of agony was horrible. My scream was louder than his. The fact that the wall bit off all ten of his fingers made me feel awful and sick to my stomach. Blood sprayed everywhere. His mumu looked like he'd participated in the scene of a murder.

"Oh no!" I shouted and pulled him back from the man-eating wall. "Are you okay?"

The question was ridiculous. He'd just gotten all his digits chomped off. Amazingly, Corny was fine with it. His smile was the widest I'd ever seen it.

"I am so sorry," I told him, forgetting to speak tele-pathically.

"Not to worry, bitch Goddess Cecily," he assured me with a bow as his hands gushed blood. "It's my honor to be of service to you."

"What happened?" Irma shouted from my pocket.

"Corny got his fingers gnawed off by the wall," Jonny supplied nonchalantly as if what had just happened was normal.

Irma laughed her furry ass off in my pocket. I was tempted to squish her, but refrained. I was already responsible for one of my people getting maimed.

Corny patted my cheek with his stumpy palm, the skin already closing over the wounds left behind by the finger-eating wall. His blood dripped down my face. I didn't wipe it away. It was all my fault.

"I'll heal shortly. This is nothing, I lost my leg in a tussle with Stella only last week!" He pointed down at his full leg. Stella winked at him. He winked back.

These Demons were lunatics. However, I was too...

Corny gestured with his raw meat-looking hand. "Dismemberment happens all the time! Follow me. I know where to go," he insisted before running down the hallway with his mumu flapping around his bare legs.

"Move it, people," I said, taking off in a sprint.

We were getting closer to Pandora and my father. I could feel it.

"I'm coming Man-mom," I whispered. "Hang on. Please. I'm going to save you. I promise."

I had no plans to break my promise.

CHAPTER FOURTEEN

"THAT'S IT," CORNY WHISPERED.

The door looked like every other door in the building.

My heart began to hammer in my chest and I took a deep breath to calm myself. My buddies were just as amped up. All five of us had bright red eyes and glowed. I checked my pocket. Irma the profane fuzzy mouse was glowing too.

We stood silently outside of a door we'd passed multiple times already. Thankfully, Corny had stopped bleeding, but his hands looked hideous. I'd seen the man behead a Demon with knitting needles and I'd been fine with it. He'd suffered pretty substantial wounds from our battle with the flaming assholes and I didn't feel guilty. However, his loss of fingers was all my fault. I was a sucky Goddess.

I pushed the thought aside and promised myself to be more careful with my people in the future. My perverted flying buddy seemed fine with the outcome. Plus, his fingers were starting to grow back. I was living in a violent world and needed to accept it fast. Corny wasn't human and neither was I.

"I sense ten fuckers in there," Stella informed us in a hushed tone.

My skin felt clammy. We'd taken twelve down earlier. Ten was two less. The math didn't make my confidence soar. Closing my eyes, I pictured Man-mom's beautiful face. My dad was my goal, this was just another part of the game. So far, we'd played to win. That wasn't changing now.

However, something felt off. If it was indeed the control room, I was shocked the Demons inside hadn't come out to kill us. They should be able to see us on the livestream. My stomach was hosting a full marching band that had just won the national championship and they were losing their collective minds.

"Is this weird?" I asked, glancing at the others.

"No," Moon said with a crazed and excited expression that made the marching band in my tummy start a drunken brawl. "An enemy is always stronger when a foe comes to them. They're the enemy. We're the foes. They think they have the upper hand right now."

"In my opinion," Jonny said. "They do."

Not what I wanted to hear.

"I call bullshit," I said, patting my pocket. We had a secret weapon named Irma. If what I'd been told was accurate about Demons and mice, this might be the least bloody battle we would ever fight.

"Should I incinerate the door?" Moon asked, gathering spit in her mouth.

"Absolutely not," I told her. *"If we burn down the control*

room, it's of no use to us. The goal is to eliminate the enemy and figure out the shitty whore's location from the feed."

"Holy crap," Moon said with a quick bow. "I'm glad you're in charge and not me."

"No shit," Irma shouted from my pocket. "It's stuffy in here. Get this fucking party started!"

I gave my army a curt nod and a smile that I hoped looked more confident than I felt. Reaching out, I tried to turn the knob.

"*Crap. It's locked,*" I muttered.

"We need the key," Jonny said. "Check under the mat. That's where spares are usually kept."

Stella punched him in the head. "There is no mat, dumbass."

Jonny's intelligence had been greatly overexaggerated.

"We could knock," Corny suggested.

My pocket heated up. I wasn't sure if Irma had taken a pee or if I was about to spontaneously combust. Quickly reaching in, my fingertips landed on the box of toothpicks. I almost passed out with relief. Candy Vargo's advice echoed loudly in my brain—*wood might not be as good as metal, but in a pinch, it works just as good. Don't lose those. They're good for pickin' things if you know what I mean.*

I didn't know what she meant then, but I did now.

"I love you Candy Vargo," I said, pulling the gold foil box out of my pocket. It vibrated in my hand.

"I thought you were into Abaddon," Moon said, confused. "You guys are a three-some with Candy Vargo?"

I ignored her.

Slowly, I opened the box. I expected to see wood. I

wasn't wrong, but the toothpicks weren't the run-of-the-mill Candy usually chewed on. They were a shimmering gold. I'd picked a few locks in the movies, but never in real life. There was no time to start being a criminal like today.

"Back up," I warned my group telepathically. *"Not sure how this is going to go."* If the lock was somehow booby-trapped, I didn't want to dismember any more of my team. I was their Goddess—their leader. I was a badass. If anyone was going to lose a hand this time, it was me. Of course, that would suck, but as I'd seen with my own eyes, appendages grew back.

It took all of one minute and thirty seconds to pick the lock. It took five seconds to open the door. It took less than a second to realize all ten flaming assholes had enchanted machetes aimed at us and were ready for some decapitation.

"In the name of the glorious Goddess Pandora, you will die violently," the one in the middle of the group roared, causing the entire building to shake.

"We're so dead," Jonny muttered.

"Not yet," I hissed and grabbed Irma from my pocket.

I kissed her furry head, held her high for the sons of bitches to see then gently put her on the floor.

"Do your thing, Irma," I instructed.

"My fucking pleasure, bitch," she squeaked as she scurried across the floor to the horrified Demons.

Chaos like I'd never seen ensued.

The screams were loud and bloodcurdling. The tears of horror and fear were unexpected. The ten enormous machete-wielding bad guys sounded like twelve-year-old girls at a Taylor Swift concert. It was fast. It was bloody. It was gory. It was really hard to watch. The only reason I did was to make sure Irma didn't get stepped on or die.

In their terrified haste to get away from a tiny mouse, the ten Demons in the control room literally obliterated each other. Heads flew, appendages were ripped from bodies and guts oozed. The squishing noises mixed with the shrieking were stomach churning. Moon cheered like she was watching a high stakes prize fight. Corny gasped, giggled and pointed at the action with his newly grown fingers. Stella cackled and joined Moon in the cheering section. Jonny snapped his fingers, conjured up some popcorn and sat down to watch the show.

Irma was having the time of her life. Her squeaky foul mouth was running the entire time she was. Twice she almost bit it. I was sure she was a goner when a head exploded right next to her, but Irma just shook it off and kept up her reign of terror.

If I'd ever read this scene in a script, I would have laughed and tossed it in the garbage for being beyond unrealistic. It was the stupidest thing anyone in their right mind could have come up with. The phrase, the truth is stranger than fiction applied here.

It was over so fast it was difficult to believe that it had even happened. However, the piles of heads and guts were proof that it had.

"And that's how it's done, bitches," Irma announced as she shifted back into her human form.

"Holy Hell." I shook my head. "That was insane."

Irma just grinned and bowed. She received a rousing round of applause from all.

"Monitors. Now," Stella said, running over to the bank of TV screens lining the wall.

She expertly avoided the gore on the ground. I wasn't as talented and ended up with something gooey and green on my shitkickers. I swallowed back the bile in my throat and focused on the important stuff.

We were alive.

Irma hadn't gotten squished.

The flaming assholes had eliminated themselves.

Win. Win. Win.

It was time to end the game.

"Are there cameras in here?" Stella asked, looking around.

It was an excellent question. "Cameras reveal."

Nothing happened. That was good. We couldn't be seen or heard right now. Pandora didn't yet know that we'd destroyed her men and were still alive. It was a rare advantage for us in the psychotic scenario.

"There," Jonny snarled, pointing to a monitor. "The shitty whore is in what looks like a damn throne room."

Moon growled deep in her throat. "I despise her. Call me crazy, but I'd swear I can smell the shitty whore from here."

Corny sniffed the air. "Well, you're definitely crazy, but I too am imagining I can smell the sickly-sweet scent."

Irma, still on a high after singlehandedly eliminating ten flaming assholes while in rodent form, sniffed the air, gagged and then puked. "Not imagining," she said, spitting then wiping her mouth. "The shitty whore was obviously in the control room at some point recently."

Normally, when someone hurled, I was tempted to join.

Not today. The sheer amount of detached body parts lying around had toughened up my gag reflexes.

I turned my attention to the monitors and glared with rage at Pandora sitting atop a shimmering silver throne. Her stunning physical beauty belied putrid insides. There was an icy evilness to her that stole my breath. My father was chained like an animal and lying on the floor in front of her. He looked near death. There was a well-armed Demon on either side of her. However, we didn't have visual access to the whole room. It could be filled with her people.

"Okay bitches," Irma said, staring at the screen with naked hatred. "We know the shitty whore is in the building. But I'm not sure how we're gonna find her."

She might not be sure, but I was...

It hit me like a ton of bricks. I grabbed a chair and sat because my knees were about to give out. Fate was set. Destiny was mine to mold. Corny Crackers, Stella Stevens, Jonny Jones, Moon Sunny Swartz and Irma Stoutwagon had been destined to be in my life. They were meant to be my people and I was meant to be their Goddess. I believed it as truth. Destiny was ours to create. We were molding our destiny together as a team. As for faith... I had faith in me and in my deranged people.

The party had started and we were about to crash it.

Snapping my fingers, I conjured up some kneepads. Handing them to Stella, I kissed her Botoxed forehead. "Do you smell the shitty whore?"

Her eyes grew wide. The nutty Demon threw her head back and laughed. She pulled on the kneepads and got down on all fours. It was somewhat disturbing to watch her circle the room and sniff the air like a dog, but at the same time, I'd never seen anything quite as lovely.

"Her ass truly is fabulous," Jonny commented, admiring Stella's backside as she began to trot.

"If I went that way, I'd have a total lady-boner right now," Moon agreed.

"Hush," I admonished them as Stella began to growl and yip.

Her ass wiggled a mile a minute and she barked.

"Is this normal?" I asked Corny.

"Oh yes," he assured me. "If she wants to hump your leg, let her. Otherwise, she bites. Are you up to date on your tetanus shots?"

I nodded and got up on the chair. While I was pretty sure a dog bite required rabies shots, I wasn't going to debate Corny. Stella wasn't a real dog even though her behavior suggested otherwise. However, getting humped or bitten right now wasn't on my to-do list.

"Listen to me, everyone," I said as we watched Stella lift her leg and pee in the corner of the room. "We're going to let Pandora believe we've turned on each other."

I angled my head away from Stella when it looked like she was going to take a dump.

"Why?" Jonny asked. "You're our bitch Goddess."

"I am. Forever," I promised him. "But the end game is getting my dad out of here alive. The best way to do it is to let her believe you're repledging your loyalty to her. As soon as you have her trust, get my dad and haul ass out of here."

Corny was perturbed. "Is this part of a fictional script?"

"Yes," I said quickly. "You're acting. Saving my dad is the climax of the movie. You'll be the hero."

"I'm a wonderful actor," Corny said. "What's the plot of the scene?"

"I'm writing it as we go—pulling it out of my ass," I told him truthfully.

"Ass plots get Oscars," Jonny told me with a thumbs up.

I returned the gesture. We were not in a movie. We were living a real and potentially deadly life—with stress on the word *real*. When in the Land of Pretend it was best to buy all the way in. "We're definitely getting an Oscar."

"Hell to the YES!" Moon shouted.

"Stella's done with her dump. She's moving," Irma yelled as Stella raced out of the control room and into the hallway.

"Go, go, go!" I yelled.

I didn't have to ask twice. My people were excellent with direction.

It was shocking how fast Stella could move on all fours. We had to sprint to keep up.

"Separate from me when we enter the room," I instructed as we ran like the wind. *"As your Goddess, I expect each of you to be nominated for an Oscar for your performance. Am I clear?"*

"Yes!" they yelled.

Stella jerked to a halt in front of a door. We almost fell over each other as we put on the brakes. I smiled at my Demons. They smiled back.

I grabbed the handle of the door and turned it. In the immortal words of Bob Fosse via Roy Scheider's mouth, I quoted one of my favorite movies of all time. *"It's showtime, folks."*

CHAPTER FIFTEEN

"Wait," Stella hissed, getting back to her feet and brushing herself off. She closed her eyes and wiggled her hips. "I sense six flaming assholes in there not counting the shitty whore and your father."

"*Is she stupid?*" I asked. Pandora had obviously watched the smackdown we'd had with her assassins a short and bloody time ago. A smart Demon would have reinforced the troops. Not to mention, she knew we were right outside of her door. The whirring of the cameras was loud.

"That's a given," Jonny whispered. "Her power and ego know no bounds. Las Vegas and the greater state of Nevada are her territories. She feels almighty here."

"Aesop," Moon said.

It was an odd non sequitur. I glanced over at her in confusion.

"He was a Greek storyteller," she explained.

"*I know that,*" I said. "*Is there a reason you brought him up?*"

"Fabulous guy," Corny commented with a nod. "Great drinking buddy."

I was reminded again of how long the company I was keeping had lived. I pushed the hard-to-imagine concept away and focused on Moon. *"What about Aesop?"*

"He said, the smaller the mind, the greater the conceit."

Irma added her two cents. "He also stated, conceit may bring about one's own downfall."

"Sage words," Stella said, patting both Irma and Moon on their backs. "I'd like to take a vote."

What the heck was happening here? We had a mission to accomplish. *"Vote?"* I asked in a stressed tone.

"Yes," she said. "I vote that we call our movie, *Aesop's Badass Demons Kick the Shitty Whore's Ass.*"

"Umm... that's a really long title," I told her with a wince.

"How about *Aesop's Assholes?*" Jonny suggested. "The alliteration is nice and the bitch Goddess Cecily is pulling the plot out of her ass."

"Oscar-worthy," Corny announced. "I love it."

I blew out a frustrated raspberry. *"Fine. Aesop's Assholes for the win. Happy?"*

"Very," Irma said. "Way better to star in *Aesop's Assholes* than be the spokeswoman for vaginal itch cream." She gave Moon the stink eye and a middle finger salute.

Moon returned the rude gesture with a grin.

I laughed. I couldn't help it. These whackadoos had lessened my stress. I wasn't sure if that was their intention or a by-product of their weirdness. Didn't matter. The result was welcome.

"Aesop did so love to get gussied up," Corny said.

My never-ending curiosity perked up. Plus, Candy
Vargo had said there were no stupid questions. That was up
for debate, but whatever. *"Gussied up?"*

"Loved a little make up," Corny explained with a giggle.
"Especially lip rouge. He wore it well!"

A zing of energy shot through me at his admission.
Candy Vargo for the win. There were *no* stupid questions.
And also, a big shout out to Shiva for the makeup
weapons. Becoming her semi-hostile BFF was on the to-do
list.

"Do you have your lipsticks?" I asked, checking my pocket
for mine. It was there.

My Demons nodded.

*"Six flaming assholes. Six lipsticks. On my command, we use
them on her flunkies. It'll give us a better chance at survival."*

"That's suspect," Stella said. "I detect a hole in the plot."

"Tell me," I said. We were working as a team. While they
might be questionable actors, I wasn't a full-time writer.

"If we attack them with the ipsticklay, it will look like we
are on uoryay idesay. The shitty whore will not believe our
oyaltylay is to erhay."

I couldn't believe I followed that, but I did. And she was
correct. The lipstick maneuver was a dead giveaway that we
were working together.

I racked my brain and came up with a rewrite on the
scene. Pulling it out of my ass was an understatement.
*"Okay... Moon, you hum quietly on my command. Let them come
at us without provocation. Make it look like self-defense then
throw yourselves on Pandora's mercy. Get close to my dad and get
him out of here."*

"Genius," Corny congratulated me. "Am I still the one chosen to transport your father?"

I paused for a moment. *"Yes,"* I told him, but I left out a big plot twist. When Corny had my dad, they were all leaving. This was my fight and they weren't going to die for me.

They were not going to be happy, but I was the Goddess and the director *of Aesop's Assholes*. My word was law. I was looking at the big picture.

"Are we ready?" I asked.

"Hell to the yes," Moon answered.

I went straight to my overused saying. It applied perfectly. *"Let's get this party started."*

And we did.

I'D SEEN THE IMAGE OF PANDORA AND MAN-MOM ON THE monitors, but nothing could have prepared me for the real thing. My dad's breathing was labored and his skin was ashen. We made eye contact and he weakly shook his head. He wanted me to leave. That wasn't happening. The fury that bubbled up inside me made me want to rip the Demon Goddess limb from limb. Rational thought was almost impossible.

"You're a fucking bitch," Irma snarled at me and punctuated it with an electrical volt.

Pandora laughed. It was slimy and made my skin crawl. However, I was wildly grateful to Irma Stoutwagon. She sensed my distress and zapped me out of it. Literally.

"Screw you," I hissed back at her. "It's time for me to end all of you so I win the prize."

The flaming assholes guarding Pandora bared their teeth. I was pretty sure they were smiling at the antics, but it was terrifying.

"I'm winning," Moon shouted, throwing daggers like confetti. "All of your pathetic asses are grass."

"In your dreams," Stella growled, punching Moon in the head and sending her flying.

The shitty whore clasped her hands in delight. A blood-bath was clearly her idea of a good time. Her lackeys enjoyed the show as well. Violence was held in high regard.

It was time to get the audience involved.

"Moon, hum," I directed as I dropped kicked Corny into Jonny.

The tune was barely audible over the shouts and vicious insults from me and my people, but it did the trick. The flaming assholes' gazes went blank, and they began to advance.

"Stop!" Pandora commanded. "I want them to end each other. Better for ratings."

They didn't listen. The pull of Moon's song was too much.

The battle grew vicious. I'd taken a claw to the face but had kicked the flaming asshole's balls up into his esophagus. It only stopped him for thirty seconds. He came at me like a nuclear weapon. All of my people were bleeding and a few body parts had been ripped off. I wasn't sure who was missing appendages. There was no time to assess the situation without getting decapitated. That scene wasn't in this movie.

We'd battled long enough to make it look real.

"Lipsticks. NOW," I shouted in their minds.

On cue, Corny, Jonny, Stella, Irma, Moon and I tased the flaming assholes. They went down with loud thuds. Pandora's confusion at the turn of events set her off. She glowed a blinding silver and grabbed my father by the neck.

"What is happening?" she bellowed as she began to choke the life out of Bill Bloom.

"Beg for mercy. NOW," I directed.

I took back thinking they were bad actors. My ragtag crew gave Oscar-worthy performances.

"Oh, beautiful Goddess Pandora," Irma cried out, throwing herself at Pandora's feet. She was missing a leg and an arm. "I beg of you to take me back. I worship you. I have lived in agony and devastation without you."

"You killed my most trusted generals," she hissed, electrocuting Irma.

"No," Irma screamed, writhing on the ground in pain. "They're not dead, just incapacitated. I swear. It was self-defense. You saw it."

Pandora considered Irma's words as she squeezed harder on my father's neck. It took effort I didn't know I possessed to not stop the scene and end her. Abaddon had told me I wasn't capable of ending her. I knew with all my heart he was wrong.

"My Goddess Pandora," Corny said in a trembling voice I'd never heard him use. "I am your humble servant. I don't care about winning the prize. I just want to win back your trust."

He crawled on all fours to her feet. She kicked him in the head with her stiletto-clad heels, but he crawled back for more.

Jonny, Moon and Stella followed their fellow actors' leads and begged for forgiveness. The shitty whore bought it hook, line and sinker.

I stood across the room separate from my people. I schooled my face in an expression of disdain for the weak Demons who pled for her acceptance at her feet.

Pandora's gaze met mine. Her eyes narrowed to slits... then she smiled. "Guess you lose, Cecily Bloom. The prize goes to my people." She waved her hand. "What say you, we turn off the cameras and let the end play out a mystery?"

The whir of the cameras ceased. My stomach cramped. Abaddon, Lilith and Dagon could no longer see the feed. If they came too early, Man-mom would die. If they came too late, I would.

The heinous Goddess tossed my father to the Demons groveling at her feet. She was so focused on me, she didn't see their grins of delight. Once I spotted Man-mom wrapped in Corny's embrace, I gave the final direction to the actors in *Aesop's Assholes*. The movie would continue, but their roles were being retired. I didn't know how the film would end, but I knew how the current scene was about to play out.

"*Plot twist,*" I said in a brook-no-bullshit tone. "*All of you are leaving now. Pandora wants me, not you. You're my people and I won't let you die.*"

The looks of shock and distress on my little army's faces were real.

"No, negotiating," I said sternly. *"The minute Corny leaves with my dad, the jig is up. You will obey me. I'm the director and your Goddess. If I bite it, tell Abaddon I love him. Send Candy Vargo a thank you note for the toothpicks and for believing that I was a badass from the get-go. Tell my dad, my brother and dead Uncle Joe that I'll try to come back as a ghost. Tell my agent Cher that I want her to represent all of you. Let Fifi and Ophelia know that they can have my house and get Fifi some earplugs to block out Ophelia's snoring. I'm proud to call you my friends. You're truly amazing Demons. It's an honor to be your Goddess. And most importantly, hug Lilith and tell her it's from me. She'll understand."*

Moon had tears running down her face. Even with the Botox, I could see Stella was devastated. Corny held my dad close and nodded in respect to me.

Irma couldn't contain herself. "That's a fuck ton to remember, bitch," she shrieked. "I'm not good at memorization."

"I'm an excellent thespian," Jonny yelled. "I have taken mental note of everything. It shall be done."

"What are you babbling about?" Pandora demanded, electrocuting them. "You will speak when you are spoken to or it will end badly… for you. Kill the human," she insisted, staring daggers at the Demons surrounding her. "Prove your loyalty to me. It will be icing on the cake for Cecily Bloom to watch her father die."

"Leave. Immediately," I commanded.

In a puff of red shimmering mist, they disappeared with my father cradled safely in Corny's arms.

Pandora's expression of utter shock would have been funny in another time and on another planet. "Well, aren't you the clever one, Cecily Bloom," she purred with venom dripping off of each over-enunciated word. "I didn't realize you were that deviously smart."

It was just her and me. I crossed my fingers and sent good vibes out into the Universe that backup was about to arrive. Man-mom was safe. It was time for all of Hell to rain down on Pandora.

For a hot sec, I considered taking a hard left in the plot and weaving in the shitty movie I'd done called *You're Not My Mother*. It had come to mind when I was at Candy Vargo's big white mansion. Had that been a sign? In the crappy B movie, I'd successfully convinced the nightmare of a woman who'd kidnapped me that I was on her side. I'd kept her going until the police arrived.

Pandora wasn't that stupid. She'd never believe I'd defect to her side no matter how good of an actress I was. However, most narcissists loved to talk about themselves. If I could get her talking, I'd buy some time.

"How did you get out of the time-out?" I questioned.

Her brow raised. She refused to speak.

Compliment the ego… "Impressive. Candy Vargo isn't someone who makes many mistakes. Your power must eclipse hers."

I didn't believe that for a second, but Pandora took the bait. She was thrilled.

"No one can trap me," she snarled. "I am the Goddess Pandora. I'm more powerful than all."

"Seems that way," I said, snapping my fingers and producing a chair. I sat down and crossed my legs.

She was taken aback at my casual demeanor.

"What do you think you're doing?" she hissed.

I shrugged and smiled. More likely than not, I was about to die. She knew it and I knew it. I'd give her a run for her money, but she was a gazillion years old and I was forty. The odds were not in my favor. "Well, since I'm about to bite it, I figured I'd get a few questions answered first. You have a problem with that?"

She wavered for a moment. With a wiggle of her fingers, she repaired her throne and sat down. "Your bravery is surprising."

"That's a compliment coming from you," I told her flatly.

She wasn't sure if I was being serious or sarcastic. I didn't help her out. "How did you learn of my existence?"

"Wouldn't you like to know," she sneered.

"Actually, yes. That's why I asked."

She was thrown easily. I wasn't kissing her ass. I wasn't afraid of her either. She didn't know what to do with the situation at hand. I felt a sudden sense of peace. I wouldn't die as a coward. I wouldn't beg for my life. That would bring her too much pleasure. It was devastating to think that I would never see Man-mom, Uncle Joe and Sean again, but I knew they'd be fine. My death would ensure their safety.

When I pictured Abaddon's handsome face, my heart broke. I loved him and he loved me. The only solace I had was that we'd cleared up the miscommunication. He'd be okay too. He had to be.

And Lilith… it ate at me that I hadn't hugged her. I'd wanted to but held back. It was a good lesson in not leaving things undone. It was too late now. In another moment of clarity, I realized I would have done the same as she'd done if the roles were reversed and she was my daughter. She loved me enough to let me live. It was a selfless act. I hoped to Hell and back that when I died, I could come back as a ghost like Uncle Joe. Telling my mom I loved her too would be one of the first things I did.

"Do you not recall who told you about me?" I queried.

"Of course, I do," she snapped. "She's dead."

My brows shot up. I knew who it was. Rhoda Spark—the Demon who had kidnapped Abaddon when he was weak then handed him over to Pandora. She pretended to be loyal to Lilith, but lied. She'd been on Team Pandora all along. Unfortunately, the reward for her blind faith in evil had been the reason for her demise. She'd annoyed Pandora and died violently at her hand because of it.

"Rhoda Spark," I said aloud.

"Correct." Pandora cracked her neck, stretched her arms, and finished with a yawn. "I'm getting bored and itching to murder you. You can have one last question."

"And you will answer it?" I challenged.

She rolled her eyes and waited.

No question was stupid… "Is Pandora's box a real thing?"

For only the briefest second the vile woman's eyes went wide with fear. It was so fleeting it could have been easily

missed. I didn't miss things like that. Human nature fascinated me. From an early age, I'd studied people. I'd always
thought I did it because I was an actress. Now, I wondered if
fate had something else in store for me with that particular
talent.

"Answer the question, Pandora."

She eyed me like I was an insect she was about to swat.
"The box exists. However, you're going to take that secret to
the grave, Cecily Bloom." She stood up and tossed her
waist-length raven-black hair over her shoulder. "I was
going to kill you slowly, but you pulled one over on me with
those deplorable Demons. For that, I shall reward you with
a quick demise."

"Am I supposed to thank you for that?" I asked.

She hissed and growled like an animal. Apparently, it
was okay for her to be a nasty bitch, but she didn't like it
when the favor was returned.

Too bad, so sad.

The air in the room grew frigid and a sickly-sweet
scented wind whipped through. Pandora clapped her hands
and produced her purple fire sword. I smiled. I wasn't going
down without a fight. I held my hands out and produced
two.

She was not pleased.

"Get ready to die, Cecily Bloom," she bellowed.

The building shook with her rage. I stood my ground
and waited for her to come to me. Dagon had said there was
strength in stillness. I was going to take his advice.

The building continued to tremble. Chunks of the

ceiling fell to the floor and the silver throne Pandora had sat upon erupted into flame.

"Stop it," she ground out. "I will not be so kind with your death if you defy me."

I wasn't doing it, but that was for me to know and for her to never find out.

When lighting fixtures exploded, all of my wishes came true. Lilith, Abaddon and Dagon appeared in a hail of black glitter and silver mist. Pandora's fury at the twist in the scene was only eclipsed by my mother's.

"You're cheating," Pandora screamed at me with spittle coming out of her mouth.

"That's rich coming from you, shitty whore," I shot back.

The vicious Goddess waved her hand. In a flash of lightning and a crash of thunder, at least fifty flaming assholes appeared. The smile on her lips was psychotic. "Kill Cecily Bloom!"

Lilith, Dagon, Abaddon and I fought the army of evil with all we had... and we had a lot. My mother was a freaking killing machine. She was balletic, precise and terrifying. For the most part, the flaming assholes avoided her. They knew who she was. Dagon was no slouch, but Abaddon fought like a crazed animal.

Blow by blow. Electrocution by electrocution. It was a bloody mess. I'd lost part of my left hand but was still able to grip my sword.

Pandora stood back and watched. Her cowardice was astounding. I might die, but she was going down.

The enemy went from fifty down to twelve quickly. However, the last dozen were determined.

"Cecily, leave," Lilith yelled over the ruckus. "Now."

I wanted to obey her. I really did, but I couldn't. This was my battle. I needed to fight it. "Not until she's back in her box," I shouted.

Everything that came next happened fast, but I would replay it in slow motion for the rest of my days. Pandora began to lob explosive fireballs. I screamed in agony when one hit my leg. I refused to look down to see if my leg was still there. The searing pain made me come close to throwing up. Moving away from the sizzling fire, I realized that even though I had third-degree burns or worse, I could still stand. I kept my eyes on Pandora's hands while trying to defend myself from her Demons.

Abaddon was at my side immediately. In the millisecond it took for me to acknowledge him, I saw a flaming asshole come up behind him wielding a fiery sword.

"Duck," I shouted at the love of my life.

Abaddon escaped being beheaded, but Pandora saw her opening. The ball of fire she hurled at me was massive, deadly and had my name all over it. I tried to dodge it, but my leg hindered my escape. The aggressive push from my right side sent me flying into Abaddon. The explosion was brutal. The building creaked on its foundation.

"What have you done?" Dagon roared in a voice so furious, I felt lightheaded.

"It's not my fault," Pandora shrieked, having a panic attack.

The Goddess pulled on her hair and ran her sharp nails down her arms leaving behind trails of oozing blood. I didn't understand what was happening... until I did.

Lilith lay collapsed on the floor where I had been only moments ago. Her beautiful body was broken and battered. The light was gone. Her life was gone. She bled profusely from her mouth and her chest wasn't moving.

The realization was hard to comprehend. It didn't make any sense, but the proof was in front of me. She died for me. My mother had brought me into this world, and now she'd sacrificed herself to keep me in it. This was all wrong.

I'd never seen red in my life. I'd heard about it but had never experienced it until now. My body heated up like a roaring furnace. My tongue felt like steaming hot sandpaper and my vision blurred with hatred. With a scream of rage so raw I was sure my throat was bleeding, I slashed my hands through the air. The last twelve flaming assholes combusted into flames while screaming in agony. The six who had been stunned by the lipsticks exploded as well. Good riddance to horrible rubbish. I smiled. It didn't reach my eyes.

"Eighteen down," I hissed at Pandora. "One to go. Get ready to die, shitty whore."

I ran at her with inhuman speed in a fit of all-consuming anger. My purple fire swords were aimed at her neck. She would pay, and I would exact the payment.

I'd never told my mother I loved her. I'd never hugged her. Now I'd never get the chance.

As I swung my swords with all my might, Pandora disappeared in a blast of black glitter. I fell to the ground from the intensity of my blows that hadn't even touched her. I stared in shock at the ground where she'd stood only moments ago.

"No, no, no," I cried out.

Abaddon's arms around me from behind felt safe and loving. I pushed him away. I didn't deserve safe and loving. My mother had died because of me.

I stood and approached her body slowly. The feeling of wanting to peel off my skin and cry forever consumed me. I sucked it back. Dagon wept as he stood guard over his Goddess's body. Abaddon wept as well.

I was so distraught the tears wouldn't come.

Getting down on my knees, I wrapped my arms around my mother the way I should have yesterday and the day before. I hugged her lifeless body close and breathed in her scent. The tears came naturally as my mind raced with all the things I'd miss without her here.

"I was supposed to teach you how to drive," I whispered brokenly. "You're a terrible driver."

I tried to wipe the blood from her face but just smeared it. Abaddon gently touched my back. It felt right and I didn't pull away.

"I never told her I loved her," I choked out, still desperately trying to clean her up with the sleeve of my shirt. "She told me she loved me, and I didn't say anything."

"She knew," Abaddon said softly.

I shook my head. "But I didn't tell her. I'll never get to tell her. I called her Lilith, not Mom."

Sobs racked my body as I held on to the woman who had traded her life for mine. My guilt overwhelmed me and I wished I could go back in time. It wasn't possible. Some things were not possible no matter how much you believed or wished on stars.

"We can't stay here," Dagon finally said in a hushed and

broken-hearted tone. "It's not safe, Goddess Cecily. We must return the Goddess's body to the Darkness before she turns to dust."

I glanced over at him. He got down on his knees and bowed to me. Abaddon did the same.

"No," I said, quickly. "No. Don't."

Abaddon raised his head and stood back up. His gaze was intense, not sexual in nature at all. It made me feel out of control and breathless.

"You're the next in line, Cecily," he said. "It's fated."

I pressed my lips together so I wouldn't scream. I wasn't the Goddess of the Darkness. I was Cecily Bloom, a former child star who was about to make a comeback in a new TV series. Dagon and Abaddon had lost their damned minds if they thought I could be the Goddess of the Darkness and replace my mother.

"It's what your mother would want," Dagon said, standing up as well.

I glanced over at him like he was nuts. "She'd want a forty-year-old actress who just found out she was a Demon to run the show? Lilith might have been a shitty driver, but she wasn't insane. I'm not fit to fill her shoes."

Dagon smiled at me. It was a sad smile, but it was real. "I promise you this is what she would want. You're her daughter—her blood. You're a born Goddess. I'll be at your side every step of the way."

"As will I," Abaddon added. "I believe in you, Cecily."

I leaned in and gently kissed my mother's forehead. "I'm not sure I believe in me."

Abaddon squatted down next to me. "How about I believe in you enough for both of us?"

I gave him a weak smile and nodded.

Fate was set. Destiny was mine to mold. Shit. Life had just taken a U-turn into Hell. Literally.

Lilith's body began to glow and shimmer. Dagon gasped. Abaddon was speechless and open-mouthed.

"What's wrong?" I asked, as the delicate magic swirled around my mother and me.

Dagon shook his head. He was frantic. "I don't know what's happening."

I caught his vibe and held my mother closer. The enchantment continued to dance around us as Lilith's broken body began to fade away. In a pop of iridescent silver mist, she disappeared.

I was frozen to the spot.

"What the Hell?" Abaddon questioned in a perplexed and alarmed tone.

"I truly don't know," Dagon said as he began to pace erratically. "She should have turned to dust."

My hackles rose. "Is it Pandora? Did she steal my mother's body?"

Abaddon growled.

Dagon held up a hand. "I don't believe Pandora had anything to do with this. It was far too peaceful."

Glancing down at where my mother used to be, I felt the tears come on again. I was going to be crying for a while. "What do we do?" I asked, sniffling.

"We get out of here," Abaddon said. "We're in Pandora's territory."

"And what about her? She's supposed to be in time-out," I reminded the men.

"The Grim Reaper and the Keeper of Fate are on it," Dagon informed me. "We shall aid them as necessary."

"The box is real," I told them.

Both men's brows shot up.

"Do you know where it is?" Abaddon asked.

"No," I told him. "But you'd better believe I'm going to find it."

"I've already told you I believe in you," he said. "I have no doubt you'll find Pandora's box. And I'll be at your side when you do."

I nodded. Exhaustion made me feel dizzy. There was nothing left here that I cared about except Abaddon and Dagon. "It's time to go. I need to see Man-mom."

"As you wish, Goddess Cecily," Dagon said with another bow of respect.

The bowing was going to take some getting used to. Honestly, I liked bitch Goddess Cecily better, but would save that for another conversation. I didn't see it going over well.

Abaddon's cell phone rang. I was surprised it worked, but the shitty whore was gone. Her spells must have left with her.

He glanced down at it and tilted his head in surprise. "It's your father," he said, handing me his phone.

My stomach flipped. I couldn't take any more bad news. Quickly, I answered. "Man-mom?"

"Cecily-boo," he said. "I was so worried."

He sounded tired and happy, but his voice was rough as if he'd been crying.

"I'm fine," I lied. I wasn't sure I was going to be fine ever again. "Are you okay?"

"I am," he said, sounding strange. Not scared strange... just really strange.

"Mmkay," I said. "I'm coming home now."

"That's good, Cecily-boo. I love you," he said. "There's someone here who wants to see you."

"I love you too. Tell Sean and Uncle Joe I'm on my way," I said with a smile.

I knew I'd have to tell Man-mom about Lilith. He'd be heartbroken. I'd take him to the safe house, so he could see how much she'd always loved him... and me.

"Not Sean and Joe," he said with a silly lightness in his voice that I'd never heard.

"Should I guess?" I asked, catching his silliness.

"I don't think you'll be able to," he replied with a chuckle.

"Okay, I give up. Who's waiting to see me?"

He took a deep breath and blew it out slowly. The suspense was killing me. "Your mother. Your mother is home and this time she's here to stay."

I couldn't say a word. Dropping the phone, I started to sob. Abaddon's phone shattered into pieces. Sean and I had been worried about our dad's memory for a while. His bout with Pandora had clearly sent him over the edge. "He thinks my mother is with him."

Abaddon squinted at me then glanced over at Dagon. "Is that possible?" he asked.

"No. I don't think so," Dagon replied.

"Is it Pandora?" Abaddon ground out.

"She's in hiding," Dagon surmised. "More importantly, Bill didn't seem to be in danger. Shiva, Cher, Fifi and Ophelia are there along with Corny, Irma, Stella, Moon and Jonny. The street is also warded. There's no way for Pandora to have entered Cecily's home."

Abaddon put his hand under my chin and gently raised my tear-stained gaze to his. "I'm not sure who is with your father, but we need to find out. Are you up to it?"

I wiped my tears and lightly kissed his lips. "No. But that's never stopped me yet."

"Take my hands," Dagon urged, clearly unnerved. "We must go at once."

I had no clue who my dad thought was my mother, but whoever was messing with him and us would be very sorry shortly.

In a blast of chilly wind and glittering black mist, we headed to the next adventure.

And what an adventure it would turn out to be...

The End... for now

GO HERE FOR THE NEXT BOOK IN THE SERIES!

NEXT IN THE GOOD TO THE LAST DEMON SERIES

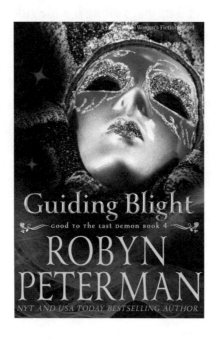

I crashed the Immortal party and it ended with a surprise encore... a big one.

I thought being a Demon sucked, but being a Demon Goddess is a whole 'nother level. Life had been so much easier when I was just a forty-year-old has-been actress trying to make a comeback in the land of Botox and BS.

For the love of everything absurd, I was just getting used to being a Demon… and BAM… all of a sudden I'm supposed to be one of the two gals in charge? I mean, being the co-star of the show is great until it involves ruling the Darkness with the evil whack job who destroyed my mother.

Pandora is a guiding blight in my world, and I plan to cancel her at all costs. With my Demon love by my side and a gaggle os Immortal nutbags along for the ride, I'll find the vicious Goddess and put her back in her box.

Ah well, fate is set. Destiny is my performance to command. I plan it improv the heck out of it. Go big or go home is my new modus operandi. Although, right now, home sounds seriously appealing. Either way, I'm strapping in and getting ready for the wildest gig yet.

ORDER GUIDING BLIGHT NOW!

EXCERPT: THE WRITE HOOK

BOOK DESCRIPTION

THE WRITE HOOK

Midlife is full of surprises. Not all of them are working for me.

At forty-two I've had my share of ups and downs. Relatively normal, except when the definition of normal changes... drastically.

NYT Bestselling Romance Author: Check
Amazing besties: Check
Lovely home: Check
Pet cat named Thick Stella who wants to kill me: Check
Wacky Tabacky Dealing Aunt: Check
Cheating husband banging the weather girl on our kitchen table: Check
Nasty Divorce: Oh yes
Characters from my novels coming to life: Umm... yes
Crazy: Possibly

Four months of wallowing in embarrassed depression should be enough. I'm beginning to realize that no one is who they seem to be, and my life story might be spinning out of my control. It's time to take a shower, put on a bra, and wear something other than sweatpants. Difficult, but doable.

With my friends—real and imaginary—by my side, I need to edit my life before the elusive darkness comes for all of us.

The plot is no longer fiction. It's my reality, and I'm writing a happy ever after no matter what. I just have to find the *write hook*.

CHAPTER 1

"I didn't leave that bowl in the sink," I muttered to no one as I stared in confusion at the blue piece of pottery with milk residue in the bottom. "Wait. Did I?"

Slowly backing away, I ran my hands through my hair that hadn't seen a brush in days—possibly longer—and decided that I wasn't going to think too hard about it. Thinking led to introspective thought, which led to dealing with reality, and that was a no-no.

Reality wasn't my thing right now.

Maybe I'd walked in my sleep, eaten a bowl of cereal, then politely put the bowl in the sink. It was possible.

"That has to be it," I announced, walking out of the kitchen and avoiding all mirrors and any glass where I could catch a glimpse of myself.

It was time to get to work. Sadly, books didn't write themselves.

"I can do this. I have to do this." I sat down at my desk

and made sure my posture didn't suck. I was fully aware it would suck in approximately five minutes, but I wanted to start out right. It would be a bad week to throw my back out. "Today, I'll write ten thousand words. They will be coherent. I will not mistakenly or on purpose make a list of the plethora of ways I would like to kill Darren. He's my past. Beheading him is illegal. I'm far better than that. On a more positive note, my imaginary muse will show his pony-tailed, obnoxious ass up today, and I won't play Candy Jelly Crush until the words are on the page."

Two hours later…

Zero words. However, I'd done three loads of laundry—sweatpants, t-shirts and underwear—and played Candy Jelly Crush until I didn't have any more lives. As pathetic as I'd become, I hadn't sunk so low as to purchase new lives. That would mean I'd hit rock bottom. Of course, I was precariously close, evidenced by my cussing out of the Jelly Queen for ten minutes, but I didn't pay for lives. I considered it a win.

I'd planned on folding the laundry but decided to vacuum instead. I'd fold the loads by Friday. It was Tuesday. That was reasonable. If they were too wrinkled, I'd simply wash them again. No biggie. After the vacuuming was done, I rearranged my office for thirty minutes. I wasn't sure how to Feng Shui, but after looking it up on my phone, I gave it a half-assed effort.

Glancing around at my handiwork, I nodded. "Much better. If the surroundings are aligned correctly, the words will flow magically. I hope."

Two hours later…

"Mother humper," I grunted as I pushed my monstrosity of a bed from one side of the bedroom to the other. "This weighs a damn ton."

I'd burned all the bedding seven weeks ago. The bonfire had been cathartic. I'd taken pictures as the five hundred thread count sheets had gone up in flame. I'd kept the comforter. I'd paid a fortune for it. It had been thoroughly saged and washed five times. Even though there was no trace of Darren left in the bedroom, I'd been sleeping in my office.

The house was huge, beautiful... and mine—a gorgeously restored Victorian where I'd spent tons of time as a child. It had an enchanted feel to it that I adored. I didn't need such an enormous abode, but I loved the location—the middle of nowhere. The internet was iffy, but I solved that by going into town to the local coffee shop if I had something important to download or send.

Darren, with the wandering pecker, thought he would get a piece of the house. He was wrong. I'd inherited it from my whackadoo grandmother and great-aunt Flip. My parents hadn't always been too keen on me spending so much time with Granny and Aunt Flip growing up, but I adored the two old gals so much they'd relented. Since I spent a lot of time in an imaginary dream world, my mom and dad were delighted when I related to actual people— even if they were left of center.

Granny and Flip made sure the house was in my name only—nontransferable and non-sellable. It was stipulated that I had to pass it to a family member or the Historical Society when I died. Basically, I had life rights. It was as if

Granny and Aunt Flip had known I would waste two decades of my life married to a jackhole who couldn't keep his salami in his pants and would need someplace to live. God rest Granny's insane soul. Aunt Flip was still kicking, although I hadn't seen her in a few years.

Aunt Flip put the K in kooky. She'd bought a cottage in the hills about an hour away and grew medicinal marijuana —before it was legal. The old gal was the black sheep of the family and preferred her solitude and her pot to company. She hadn't liked Darren a bit. She and Granny both had worn black to my wedding. Everyone had been appalled— even me—but in the end, it made perfect sense. I had to hand it to the old broads. They'd been smarter than me by a long shot. And the house? It had always been my charmed haven in the storm.

Even though there were four spare bedrooms plus the master suite, I chose my office. It felt safe to me.

Thick Stella preferred my office, and I needed to be around something that had a heartbeat. It didn't matter that Thick Stella was bitchy and swiped at me with her deadly kitty claws every time I passed her. I loved her. The feeling didn't seem mutual, but she hadn't left me for a twenty-three-year-old with silicone breast implants and huge, bright white teeth.

"Thick Stella, do you think Sasha should wear red to her stepmother's funeral?" I asked as I plopped down on my newly Feng Shuied couch and narrowly missed getting gouged by my cat. "Yes or no? Hiss at me if it's a yes. Growl at me if it's a no."

Thick Stella had a go at her privates. She was useless.

"That wasn't an answer." I grabbed my laptop from my desk. Deciding it was too dangerous to sit near my cat, I settled for the love seat. The irony of the piece of furniture I'd chosen didn't escape me.

"I think she should wear red," I told Thick Stella, who didn't give a crap what Sasha wore. "Her stepmother was an asshat, and it would show fabu disrespect."

Typing felt good. Getting lost in a story felt great. I dressed Sasha in a red Prada sheath, then had her behead her ex-husband with a dull butter knife when he and his bimbo showed up unexpectedly to pay their respects at the funeral home. It was a bloodbath. Putting Sasha in red was an excellent move. The blood matched her frock to a T.

Quickly rethinking the necessary murder, I moved the scene of the decapitation to the empty lobby of the funeral home. It would suck if I had to send Sasha to prison. She hadn't banged Damien yet, and everyone was eagerly awaiting the sexy buildup—including me. It was the fourth book in the series, and it was about time they got together. The sexual tension was palpable.

"What in the freaking hell?" I snapped my laptop shut and groaned. "Sasha doesn't have an ex-husband. I can't do this. I've got nothing." Where was my muse hiding? I needed the elusive imaginary idiot if I was going to get any writing done. "Chauncey, dammit, where are you?"

"My God, you're loud, Clementine," a busty, beautiful woman dressed in a deep purple Regency gown said with an eye roll.

She was seated on the couch next to Thick Stella, who barely acknowledged her. My cat attacked strangers and friends. Not today. My fat feline simply glanced over at the intruder and yawned. The cat was a traitor.

Forget the furry betrayer. How in the heck did the woman get into my house—not to mention my office—without me seeing her enter? For a brief moment, I wondered if she'd banged my husband too but pushed the sordid thought out of my head. She looked to be close to thirty—too old for the asshole.

"Who are you?" I demanded, holding my laptop over my head as a weapon.

If I threw it and it shattered, I would be screwed. I couldn't remember the last time I'd backed it up. If I lost the measly, somewhat disjointed fifty thousand words I'd written so far, I'd have to start over. That wouldn't fly with my agent or my publisher.

"Don't be daft," the woman replied. "It's rather unbecoming. May I ask a question?"

"No, you may not," I shot back, trying to place her.

She was clearly a nutjob. The woman was rolling up on thirty but had the vernacular of a seventy-year-old British society matron. She was dressed like she'd walked off the set of a film starring Emma Thompson. Her blonde hair shone to the point of absurdity and was twisted into an elaborate up-do. Wispy tendrils framed her perfectly heart-shaped face. Her sparkling eyes were lavender, enhanced by the over-the-top gown she wore.

Strangely, she was vaguely familiar. I just couldn't remember how I knew her.

"How long has it been since you attended to your hygiene?" she inquired.

Putting my laptop down and picking up a lamp, I eyed her. I didn't care much for the lamp or her question. I had been thinking about Marie Condo-ing my life, and the lamp didn't bring me all that much joy. If it met its demise by use of self-defense, so be it. "I don't see how that's any of your business, lady. What I'd suggest is that you leave. Now. Or else I'll call the police. Breaking and entering is a crime."

She laughed. It sounded like freaking bells. Even though she was either a criminal or certifiable, she was incredibly charming.

"Oh dear," she said, placing her hand delicately on her still heaving, milky-white bosom. "You are so silly. The constable knows quite well that I'm here. He advised me to come."

"The constable?" I asked, wondering how far off her rocker she was.

She nodded coyly. "Most certainly. We're all terribly concerned."

I squinted at her. "About my hygiene?"

"That, amongst other things," she confirmed. "Darling girl, you are not an ace of spades or, heaven forbid, an adventuress. Unless you want to be an ape leader, I'd recommend bathing."

"Are you right in the head?" I asked, wondering where I'd left my damn cell phone. It was probably in the laundry room. I was going to be murdered by a nutjob, and I'd lost my chance to save myself because I'd been playing Candy Jelly Crush. The headline would be horrifying—*Homeless-looking, Hygiene-free Paranormal Romance Author Beheaded by Victorian Psycho.*

If I lived through the next hour, I was deleting the game for good.

"I think it would do wonders for your spirit if you donned a nice tight corset and a clean chemise," she suggested, skillfully ignoring my question. "You must pull yourself together. Your behavior is dicked in the nob."

I sat down and studied her. My about-to-be-murdered radar relaxed a tiny bit, but I kept the lamp clutched tightly in my hand. My gut told me she wasn't going to strangle me. Of course, I could be mistaken, but Purple Gal didn't seem violent—just bizarre. Plus, the lamp was heavy. I could knock her ladylike ass out with one good swing.

How in the heck did I know her? College? Grad School? The grocery store? At forty-two, I'd met a lot of people in my life. Was she with the local community theater troop? I was eighty-six percent sure she wasn't here to off me. However, I'd been wrong about life-altering events before— like not knowing my husband was boffing someone young enough to have been our daughter.

"What language are you speaking?" I spotted a pair of scissors on my desk. If I needed them, it was a quick move to grab them. I'd never actually killed anyone except in fictitious situations, but there was a first time for everything.

Pulling an embroidered lavender hankey from her cleavage, she clutched it and twisted it in her slim fingers. "Clementine, *you* should know."

"I'm at a little disadvantage here," I said, fascinated by the batshit crazy woman who'd broken into my home. "You seem to know my name, but I don't know yours."

And that was when the tears started. Hers. Not mine.

"Such claptrap. How very unkind of you, Clementine," she burst out through her stupidly attractive sobs.

It was ridiculous how good the woman looked while crying. I got all blotchy and red, but not the mystery gal in purple. She grew even more lovely. It wasn't fair. I still had no clue what the hell she was talking about, but on the off chance she might throw a tantrum if I asked more questions, I kept my mouth shut.

And yes, she had a point, but my *hygiene* was none of her damn business. I couldn't quite put my finger on the last time I'd showered. If I had to guess, it was probably in the last five to twelve days. I was on a deadline for a book. To be more precise, I was late for my deadline on a book. I didn't exactly have time for personal sanitation right now.

And speaking of deadlines...

"How about this?" My tone was excessively polite. I almost laughed. The woman had illegally entered my house, and I was behaving like she was a guest. "I'll take a shower later today after I get through a few pivotal chapters. Right now, you should leave so I can work."

"Yes, of course," she replied, absently stroking Fat Stella, who purred. If I'd done that, I would be minus a finger. "It would be dreadfully sad if you were under the hatches."

I nodded. "Right. That would, umm... suck."

The woman in purple smiled. It was radiant, and I would have sworn I heard birds happily chirping. I was losing it.

"Excellent," she said, pulling a small periwinkle velvet bag from her cleavage. I wondered what else she had stored in there and hoped there wasn't a weapon. "I shall leave you with two gold coins. While the Grape Nuts were tasty, I would prefer that you purchase some Lucky Charms. I understand they are magically delicious."

"It was you?" I asked, wildly relieved that I hadn't been sleep eating. I had enough problems at the moment. Gaining weight from midnight dates with cereal wasn't on the to-do list.

"It was," she confirmed, getting to her feet and dropping the coins into my hand. "The consistency was quite different from porridge, but I found it tasty—very crunchy."

"Right... well... thank you for putting the bowl in the sink." Wait. Why the hell was I thanking her? She'd wandered in and eaten my Grape Nuts.

"You are most welcome, Clementine," she said with a disarming smile that lit up her unusual eyes. "It was lovely finally meeting you even if your disheveled outward show is entirely astonishing."

I was reasonably sure I had just been insulted by the cereal lover, but it was presented with excellent manners. However, she did answer a question. We hadn't met. I wasn't sure why she seemed familiar. The fact that she knew my name was alarming.

"Are you a stalker?" I asked before I could stop myself.

I'd had a few over the years. Being a *New York Times* bestselling author was something I was proud of, but it had come with a little baggage here and there. Some people seemed to have difficulty discerning fiction from reality. If I had to guess, I'd say Purple Gal might be one of those people.

I'd only written one Regency novel, and that had been at the beginning of my career, before I'd found my groove in paranormal romance. I was way more comfortable writing about demons and vampires than people dressed in top hats and hoopskirts. Maybe the crazy woman had read my first book. It hadn't done well, and for good reason. It was over-the-top bad. I'd blocked the entire novel out of my mind. Live and learn. It had been my homage to Elizabeth Hoyt well over a decade ago. It had been clear to all that I should leave Regency romance to the masters.

"Don't be a Merry Andrew," the woman chided me. "Your bone box is addled. We must see to it at once. I shall pay a visit again soon."

The only part of her gibberish I understood was that she thought she was coming back. Note to self—change all the locks on the doors. Since it wasn't clear if she was packing heat in her cleavage, I just smiled and nodded.

"Alrighty then..." I was unsure if I should walk her to the door or if she would let herself out. Deciding it would be better to make sure she actually left instead of letting her hide in my pantry to finish off my cereal, I gestured to the door. "Follow me."

Thick Stella growled at me. I was so tempted to flip her off but thought it might earn another lecture from Purple Gal. It was more than enough to be lambasted for my appearance. I didn't need my manners picked apart by someone with a tenuous grip on reality.

My own grip was dubious as it was.

"You might want to reconsider breaking into homes," I said, holding the front door open. "It could end badly—for you."

Part of me couldn't believe that I was trying to help the

nutty woman out, but I couldn't seem to stop myself. I kind of liked her.

"I'll keep that in mind," she replied as she sauntered out of my house into the warm spring afternoon. "Remember, Clementine, there is always sunshine after the rain."

As she made her way down the long sunlit, tree-lined drive, she didn't look back. It was disturbingly like watching the end of a period movie where the heroine left her old life behind and walked proudly toward her new and promising future.

Glancing around for a car, I didn't spot one. Had she left it parked on the road so she could make a clean getaway after she'd bludgeoned me? Had I just politely escorted a murderer out of my house?

Had I lost it for real?

Probably.

As she disappeared from sight, I felt the weight of the gold coins still clutched in my hand. Today couldn't get any stranger.

At least, I hoped not.

Opening my fist to examine the coins, I gasped. "What in the heck?"

There was nothing in my hand.

Had I dropped them? Getting down on all fours, I searched. Thick Stella joined me, kind of—more like watched me as I crawled around and wondered if anything that had just happened had actually happened.

"Purple Gal gave me coins to buy Lucky Charms," I told my cat, my search now growing frantic. "You saw her do it. Right? She sat next to you. And you didn't attack her. *Right?*"

Thick Stella simply stared at me. What did I expect? If my cat answered me, I'd have to commit myself. That option might still be on the table. Had I just imagined the entire exchange with the strange woman? Should I call the cops?

"And tell them what?" I asked, standing back up and locking the front door securely. "That a woman in a purple gown broke in and ate my cereal while politely insulting my hygiene? Oh, and she left me two gold coins that disappeared in my hand as soon as she was out of sight? That's not going to work."

I'd call the police if she came back, since I wasn't sure she'd been here at all. She hadn't threatened to harm me. Purple Gal had been charming and well-mannered the entire time she'd badmouthed my cleanliness habits. And to be quite honest, real or not, she'd made a solid point. I could use a shower.

Maybe four months of wallowing in self-pity and only living inside the fictional worlds I created on paper had taken more of a toll than I was aware of. Getting lost in my stories was one of my favorite things to do. It had saved me more than once over the years. It was possible that I'd let it go too far. Hence, the Purple Gal hallucination.

Shit.

First things first. Delete Candy Jelly Crush. Getting rid of the white noise in my life was the first step to... well, the first step to something.

I'd figure it out later.

HIT HERE TO ORDER THE WRITE HOOK!!!!!

ROBYN'S BOOK LIST

(IN CORRECT READING ORDER)

HOT DAMNED SERIES
Fashionably Dead
Fashionably Dead Down Under
Hell on Heels
Fashionably Dead in Diapers
A Fashionably Dead Christmas
Fashionably Hotter Than Hell
Fashionably Dead and Wed
Fashionably Fanged
Fashionably Flawed
A Fashionably Dead Diary
Fashionably Forever After
Fashionably Fabulous
A Fashionable Fiasco
Fashionably Fooled
Fashionably Dead and Loving It
Fashionably Dead and Demonic

The Oh My Gawd Couple
A Fashionable Disaster

GOOD TO THE LAST DEMON SERIES
As the Underworld Turns
The Edge of Evil
The Bold and the Banished
Guiding Blight

GOOD TO THE LAST DEATH SERIES
It's a Wonderful Midlife Crisis
Whose Midlife Crisis Is It Anyway?
A Most Excellent Midlife Crisis
My Midlife Crisis, My Rules
You Light Up My Midlife Crisis
It's A Matter of Midlife and Death
The Facts Of Midlife
It's A Hard Knock Midlife
Run for Your Midlife
It's A Hell of A Midlife

MY SO-CALLED MYSTICAL MIDLIFE SERIES
The Write Hook
You May Be Write
All The Write Moves
My Big Fat Hairy Wedding

SHIFT HAPPENS SERIES
Ready to Were
Some Were in Time

No Were To Run
Were Me Out
Were We Belong

MAGIC AND MAYHEM SERIES
Switching Hour
Witch Glitch
A Witch in Time
Magically Delicious
A Tale of Two Witches
Three's A Charm
Switching Witches
You're Broom or Mine?
The Bad Boys of Assjacket
The Newly Witch Game
Witches In Stitches

SEA SHENANIGANS SERIES
Tallulah's Temptation
Ariel's Antics
Misty's Mayhem
Petunia's Pandemonium
Jingle Me Balls

A WYLDE PARANORMAL SERIES
Beauty Loves the Beast

HANDCUFFS AND HAPPILY EVER AFTERS SERIES
How Hard Can it Be?
Size Matters

Cop a Feel

If after reading all the above you are still wanting more adventure and zany fun, read *Pirate Dave and His Randy Adventures*, the romance novel budding novelist Rena helped wicked Evangeline write in *How Hard Can It Be?*

Warning: Pirate Dave Contains Romance Satire, Spoofing, and Pirates with Two Pork Swords.

NOTE FROM THE AUTHOR

If you enjoyed reading *As The Bold and the Banished,* please consider leaving a positive review or rating on the site where you purchased it. Reader reviews help my books continue to be valued by resellers and help new readers make decisions about reading them.

You are the reason I write these stories and I sincerely appreciate each of you!

Many thanks for your support,
~ Robyn Peterman

Want to hear about my new releases?
Visit https://robynpeterman.com/newsletter/ and join my mailing list!

ABOUT ROBYN PETERMAN

Robyn Peterman writes because the people inside her head won't leave her alone until she gives them life on paper. Her addictions include laughing really hard with friends, shoes (the expensive kind), Target, Coke (the drink not the drug LOL) with extra ice in a Yeti cup, bejeweled reading glasses, her kids, her super-hot hubby and collecting stray animals.

A former professional actress with Broadway, film and T.V. credits, she now lives in the South with her family and too many animals to count.

Writing gives her peace and makes her whole, plus having a job where she can work in sweatpants is perfect for her.

Made in the USA
Thornton, CO
06/06/23 08:43:19